"She's a beautiful little girl."

Brent felt as if his throat was constricting again. His eyes stung, and he didn't bother trying to blink back the tears. Would he ever see her again?

"Yes, she is," he agreed quietly. His fingers tightened around the remote, but he made no move to stop the video. "I shouldn't be standing here, doing nothing. Thinking about eating. Thinking about—" His voice halted abruptly as guilt washed over his face.

"Thinking about what?" Callie half expected him to say something about killing the man who'd done this horrible thing.

She was caught completely by surprise when he quietly confessed, "You."

Dear Reader,

This is a month full of greats: great authors, great miniseries…great books. Start off with award-winning Marie Ferrarella's *Racing Against Time,* the first in a new miniseries called CAVANAUGH JUSTICE. This family fights for what's right—and their reward is lasting love.

The miniseries excitement continues with the second of Carla Cassidy's CHEROKEE CORNERS trilogy. *Dead Certain* brings the hero and heroine together to solve a terrible crime, but it keeps them together with love. Candace Irvin's latest features *A Dangerous Engagement*, and it's also the first SISTERS IN ARMS title, introducing a group of military women bonded through friendship and destined to find men worthy of their hearts.

Of course, you won't want to miss our stand-alone books, either. Marilyn Tracy's *A Warrior's Vow* is built around a suspenseful search for a missing child, and it's there, in the rugged Southwest, that her hero and heroine find each other. Cindy Dees has an irresistible Special Forces officer for a hero in *Line of Fire*—and he takes aim right at the heroine's heart. Finally, welcome new author Loreth Anne White, who came to us via our eHarlequin.com Web site. *Melting the Ice* is her first book—and we're all eagerly awaiting her next.

Enjoy—and come back next month for more exciting romantic reading, only from Silhouette Intimate Moments.

Leslie J. Wainger
Executive Editor

Please address questions and book requests to:
Silhouette Reader Service
U.S.: 3010 Walden Ave., P.O. Box 1325, Buffalo, NY 14269
Canadian: P.O. Box 609, Fort Erie, Ont. L2A 5X3

Racing
Against Time
MARIE FERRARELLA

Silhouette®

INTIMATE MOMENTS™

Published by Silhouette Books

America's Publisher of Contemporary Romance

SILHOUETTE BOOKS

ISBN 0-373-27319-3

RACING AGAINST TIME

Copyright © 2003 by Marie Rydzynski-Ferrarella

Visit Silhouette at www.eHarlequin.com

Printed in U.S.A.

Books by Marie Ferrarella in Miniseries

MARIE FERRARELLA

earned a master's degree in Shakespearean comedy, and, perhaps as a result, her writing is distinguished by humor and natural dialogue. This RITA® Award-winning author's goal is to entertain and to make people laugh and feel good. She has written over one hundred books for Silhouette, some under the name Marie Nicole. Her romances are beloved by fans worldwide and have been translated into Spanish, Italian, German, Russian, Polish, Japanese and Korean.

To
Helen Conrad,
still wonderful
after all these years

Prologue

He sat in his car and watched them.

Just as he had yesterday. And the day before that. And the day before that. Watched them and memorized their movements.

He didn't want there to be any slipups.

That was what had gotten him in trouble before. Thinking he hadn't made a mistake when he had. He'd been too confident, too sure that he was smarter than the people around him.

This time he knew better. Knew that he couldn't allow the fact that he was more intelligent than the people he was dealing with to blur his caution, his inbred sense of survival.

That had gotten away from him before, caused his downfall.

Pride went before a fall.

He still had his pride. And it was that pride he meant to avenge.

His pride and his life.

Because the man who lived in the house he was watching, whose comings and goings he had quickly committed to memory, had taken it all away from him. Taken away his life, his pride.

His daughter.

Payback time was finally here.

Very carefully he turned the key in the ignition. The vehicle he was sitting in purred to life, ready to do his bidding.

He smiled to himself as he moved the transmission shift lever into drive.

He was through waiting.

It was time to act.

Chapter 1

Brenton Montgomery didn't generally oversleep.

Quite the opposite, in fact. Former decorated Aurora police officer, former respected A.D.A. and presently, highly regarded criminal court justice, he had been blessed with an inner clock that went off anywhere from two to five minutes before the alarm clock on his nightstand. It had been that way ever since he'd had a need for an alarm clock.

But every once in a while, after he put in a particularly long night poring over briefs and struggling with his conscience over which was the right path for him to take for all parties who stood before his scarred judge's desk in criminal court, Brent discovered that sleep wouldn't come.

And then, when it finally did arrive, it brought with it an asbestos blanket that smothered him, ef-

fectively separating him from the rest of the world.
From the rest of his life.

This morning he'd rolled over in the four-poster
bed that Jennifer had selected—the bed that was the
single inanimate holdover from his brief mistake of
a marriage—and had hardly been aware of opening
his eyes. He didn't remember focusing on the clock
beside his telephone. But the instant he did, he'd sat
bolt upright as the flashing blue digital lights imprinted themselves on his brain.

Seven-fifty.

He was due in court at eight-thirty.

Brent had no memory of his trip down the front
stairs.

"I thought you'd decided to sleep in this morning,
Judge."

The statement greeted him exactly twelve minutes
later as, damp from his shower, his clothes sticking
to him as if he'd woken up in a swamp, Brent hurried
into the kitchen and past his housekeeper, Delia Culhane. The sight of his five-year-old daughter, Rachel,
sitting on a stool at the breakfast counter registered
along the perimeter of his mind. She was wearing
something blue. Maybe lavender or light purple.

"If I had intended on sleeping in, Delia, I would
have told you."

Without meaning to, Brent bit the words off
gruffly as he swung open the refrigerator and grabbed
one of the individual orange juice containers that Delia kept stocked for Rachel. There was no time for
breakfast. This was going to have to do.

It took effort to rein in his temper. He had no patience with tardiness, least of all his own. "I should have been in the car two minutes ago."

Briefcase in one hand, juice container in the other, Brent hurried out the back door to the garage where his BMW was housed, a hastily tossed goodbye hanging in the air behind him.

After he'd driven down the first long block, it occurred to him that for the first time in five years, he hadn't kissed his daughter goodbye.

He debated turning around, but there was no time. He was already going to be late.

Brent kept on driving.

"About time you got here. Everyone else is already seated at the table, eating."

Barking out the greeting to his firstborn daughter as the back door opened then closed behind her, Andrew Cavanaugh barely dragged his glance away from the professional stove that took up half of the back wall. The French toast he was preparing commanded his entire attention, although his family knew that he could have very easily prepared any one of a number of meals blindfolded and made them to mouthwatering perfection. Approaching his sixth decade, he was a better chef than he had been a police chief, and he had been a very, very good police chief.

Callie Cavanaugh slid in at the wide kitchen table beside her older brother, Shaw. She nodded at her three other siblings and removed the napkin from the center of her plate. She wasn't really hungry, but breakfast in the house where she and her brothers and sisters had grown up was a ritual. It had been ever since her father had retired from the force.

Andrew claimed it was his way of keeping track of his brood and anyone else who wanted to show up at the table for a meal. There was never a shortage of food. Or love, for that matter, though that was not always as blatantly on display as the plates were. But it was understood. You had a problem, no matter what your age, you showed up at the table. There'd be someone along to help sort things out, by and by.

All five of the Cavanaugh children had followed in their father's footsteps and joined the Aurora Police Department. Even Lorrayne, the youngest and the official family hellion had finally come around, after giving her father twelve years of grief and turning the rest of his black hair gray. The fact that all of them chose to go into law enforcement was a testament to the regard with which they held their father.

Callie took a sip from the glass of orange juice that was next to her plate. There were times when it seemed to her that everyone named Cavanaugh found their way into law enforcement eventually. Her grandfather had served, as had both of her father's brothers. The younger of the two, Brian, was currently the chief of detectives. Another brother, Mike, two years his junior, had died in the line of duty fifteen years ago. His son, Patrick, had joined the force, as well.

Only Uncle Mike's daughter, Patience, had broken away from the family mould and become a veterinarian. But even she had ties to the department. In her capacity as vet, she treated all the dogs that had been recruited into the K-9 division.

Uncle Brian's only daughter, Janelle, worked in the D.A.'s office while his sons Troy, Jarrod and Dax had all taken the long, blue path into law enforcement, as well.

"So, what kept you?" Andrew wanted to know as he placed a piece of French toast dusted with powdered sugar on Callie's plate.

She looked down at the serving. It was quite possibly the largest piece of French toast to ever have come out of a pan, but then, Andrew believed bigger was better when it came to breakfast. He knew that quite often there would be no time for lunch or possibly even dinner until the wee hours. So breakfast, he maintained, was a definite necessity for survival, and the more, the better.

"I caught every red light from the apartment to here." It was a lie, but Callie felt it could be excused. If she told her father the truth, he'd look at her with those sympathetic blue-gray eyes of his, and she wasn't up to that right now. Better sarcasm than kindness. Kindness had a way of creeping under the layers of the barriers she'd laid around herself and undermining all her hard work. She smiled prettily at him. "Wouldn't want me speeding now, would you?"

He saw right through her, the way he did all his

children. It was the sixth sense that some parents
were blessed with. Or cursed with, depending on the
point of view.

Still, he played along, knowing what saving face
was all about. More than once he'd drifted in the
same rudderless boat his daughter had occupied. And
on occasion, it came by to give him a return trip to
the land of hopelessness. The only difference was
that for him, there'd never been any real closure, no
tangible evidence to extinguish the last flicker of
hope that Rose was still alive.

"No," he agreed. "Would like to see you getting
up earlier, though, so you could make it while the
meal was still hot."

She looked down at the serving he'd just placed
before her. There was steam curling from it. "Any
hotter, Dad, and my plate'll go up in smoke." She
waited until he finished filling her coffee cup, then
reached for it. "You know, I can pour my own cup
of coffee."

Andrew stopped to top off Shaw's cup before placing the pot back on its stand. "I know. So can I."
He raised one semidark eyebrow as he fixed her with
a penetrating look. "Or would you want to deny an
old man one of the few pleasures he has left in life?"

Shaw snorted as he polished off the last of his own
breakfast. "Old man," he echoed. "That'll be the
day."

Adding a drop of cream to her pitch-black coffee,
Callie smiled at the wordplay. She picked up the cup
with both hands and took a long, deep sip. Her fa-

ther's coffee was guaranteed to get a stopped heart beating again, and this morning she knew she needed all the help she could get.

She'd barely slept, having finally drifted off, if it could be called that, somewhere around three. Memories of Kyle insisted on haunting her. Last Saturday had marked one year since his death.

Funny, she'd thought she was finally making progress, finally moving on with her life. Wrong.

Just went to show you that you could never count on anything. Other than family, she amended. The sun would stop rising in the east before she would ever stop counting on her family to come through for her.

But this wasn't the kind of thing her family could really help with. The best they could do was just silently be there for her. Support her with their presence, but not their words. Words were useless.

Callie counted on her work to take up the slack, to blanket the pain until she could handle it. So far, the pain was refusing to let itself be pushed into the background for more than a few days at a time.

It wasn't that she wanted to forget Kyle. Kyle embodied so many of the best moments of her life. She just wanted to be able to think of him without shards of glass cutting into her chest and gut, making it an effort to breathe.

That wasn't too much to ask, was it?

As if reading her mind, she felt her father's hand on her shoulder. Just a little extra pressure, nothing more. But it was enough. She smiled her thanks, grateful for his understanding. Equally grateful that he didn't verbalize anything.

And then he was on his way, back to the stove and his first love. They all knew, because he'd told them countless times, how he'd put himself through school as a short-order cook and had managed to develop into one hell of a chef over the years, whenever his career didn't put demands on him.

The stack of French toast piled on the platter beside the stove was beginning to rival the Leaning Tower of Pisa. Andrew drew over a second platter and decreased the pile, then glanced over his shoulder toward the table.

"Seconds, anyone?"

It was a misleading question. Most of them had already had seconds. By the looks of it, Clay was on thirds. Their father's cooking was far too good to resist. Callie was thoroughly convinced that even Gandhi would have been tempted to at least temporarily turn his back on his well-publicized fast to sample a little of her father's creations.

But just as Andrew asked, the sound of a beeper going off framed his words. Five sets of eyes went to the appendages they kept clipped to their belts.

A blue light highlighting a phone number was looking back at her. "Mine," Callie declared.

"And we have a winner," Andrew sighed, shaking his head.

Andrew knew she would be leaving momentarily. On the other side of the fence now, he felt the frustration that he knew his wife had had to endure every time he'd been called away from the table, or missed a meal because of the demands of his job.

He glanced accusingly at the barely touched fare on his oldest daughter's plate. The powder hadn't even faded yet. "You haven't had time to eat enough food to keep a hummingbird alive."

"They eat twice their body weight, Dad," Teri informed him as she broke off a piece of what was to become her third serving of French toast. "You wouldn't want Callie to roll out of here, would you?"

"No chance of that happening even if she ate three times her body weight," Clay, Teri's younger brother by two and a half minutes, commented. Though they were twins, they hardly looked alike. Fair, with long blond hair, Teri looked like their mother, while Clay, though not as dark as Shaw, had their father's black Irish look.

Callie held her hand up for silence as she dug out her cell phone. She might as well not have wasted the effort. There was an annoying message on her LCD screen. She frowned. "No signal."

"Must be Clay's magnetic personality, interfering," Teri cracked. "Hey," she protested as Clay helped himself to the remainder of her toast. She pulled back her plate, but it was too late. The right flank of her French toast had been victimized.

Andrew pretended to shake his head. "Ah, the sound of squabbling children, how could I have forgotten what that was like?"

All but two of his children had moved out, but the

apartment Clay had been subletting from an aspiring actor had suddenly been reclaimed by its owner when the latter returned from the east coast. That left Clay without a place to stay. Temporarily.

Temporarily had already woven its way into two months without any visible signs of terminating. And Andrew, secretly, couldn't have been happier even though he said nothing out loud to confirm it.

"Hey, if you didn't want them coming around, Dad, you'd stop leaving food out for them to find," Lorrayne pointed out.

"Respect your elders, Squirt," Shaw told her just before he drank deeply of his third cup of leaded coffee.

Rayne lifted her chin defensively, her blue-gray eyes narrowing beneath her bangs. "Just who are you calling Squirt?"

Knowing that the only way to quiet this crowd was to arm herself with a handful of tranquilizer darts and use them effectively, Callie crossed into the living room to get away from the din before placing her call to the number registered on her beeper. A glance at the screen told her the transmission signal had returned.

Holding one hand over her ear as she turned away from the breakfast noise, she quickly hit the keypad numbers with her thumb.

"This is Cavanaugh," she said the second she heard someone pick up on the other end. "You paged me?"

"Better get down here, Callie."

She recognized the voice. It belonged to the man she'd been partnered with until recently. Seth Adams. The man had made detective five years before she had and had resented being "saddled" with her. He'd thought nepotism had placed her where she was. He'd soon learned that it was aptitude that had gotten her her badge, nothing more, nothing less. Still, they blended together like oil and water. The captain agreed that a separation was in order.

"What's up?" she wanted to know.

"We've got a dead woman on the sidewalk. Looks like she was struck and thrown by a car."

She waited for something more to follow. When it didn't, she asked, "Hit-and-run?"

"Absolutely."

It didn't make sense to her. "Vehicular manslaughter. How's that my territory?"

Callie dealt with the living, not the dead. Specifically, with searching for missing persons. It was a department that was near and dear to her father's heart. Fifteen years ago, her mother had gotten into her car and driven away. She never came back. The car was eventually found submerged in a lake twenty miles north of Aurora, but no amount of searching had ever turned up her body.

Her father never gave up the hope that someday Rose Cavanaugh would come walking back into the house she'd stormed out of in the wake of an argument her father never stopped blaming himself for. In some small way, Callie felt that by working in missing persons she kept up her father's hope that her mother was still alive.

"She wasn't alone, Callie. From all appearances, the woman had a little girl with her. The first cop on the scene went through the dead woman's wallet. Delia Anne Culhane. Judge Brenton Montgomery's housekeeper." He paused for a moment, letting the words sink in. "The missing kid is his daughter."

A knot came out of nowhere and tightened itself in the pit of her stomach as she recognized the name.

"I'll be right there." Hanging up, Callie turned around. Her father was standing just shy of the threshold, watching her. He couldn't have gotten very much from her side of the conversation, she thought. She debated saying something to him. He knew Montgomery better than she did. Another time, she decided. "I've got to get going."

It was then that she noticed her father was holding a brown paper bag in his hand. Full if the bulge in the middle was any indication.

He held it out to her. "Packed you a lunch." He smiled, the character lines about his eyes crinkling. "In case you get hungry one of these days."

She knew he meant well, but she wasn't thirteen anymore, being sent off to school. "Dad—"

Taking her hand, he closed her fingers around the top of the bag. "Humor me. I've been both mother and father to this bunch for fifteen years." His smile took twenty years off his age. "These parental urges get hard to fight sometimes."

As always, she retreated from the line of skirmish.

She'd learned long ago to pick her fights, and this wasn't worth more than a few words. She grinned at him, nodding at the bag. "Will I like it?"

The expression on Andrew's face was incredulous, as if he couldn't believe she had to ask. "Is the pope Catholic?"

"Last I checked." She paused to kiss his cheek. "Thanks, Dad." The words had nothing to do with the lunch he'd tucked into her hand, and everything to do with the care he'd spent raising her right.

Embarrassed, Andrew waved her on her way. "Go. They're waiting on you." He guessed at the caller. "Tell Adams I said hello."

Callie stopped. She hadn't told him who was on the phone. "How is it you know everything?"

He gave her a crooked grin. "I'm old. I'm supposed to know everything. I've got it in writing. Now get going before the crime scene gets contaminated."

If it hasn't already been, she thought. Nodding, Callie hurried out the door she'd used less than ten minutes ago.

An hour and a half later, Callie paused outside the closed doors of the courtroom. Gathering courage and the right words.

There were no right words. Not for this.

The corridor on the second floor was mostly empty. Courts were in session behind the black double doors that lined both sides of the long hallway. If she listened intently, she could swear that she could almost hear various lives being altered.

And behind this particular set of doors some family's life was being rearranged by a man known to be both just and fair. And not easily swayed by pretense. A dark, sober man who brooked no nonsense, stood for no lies. And had had his share of grief.

And she was going to add to it.

Callie let out a long breath, then took in another, centering herself. She'd just left the scene of the accident.

The scene of the crime, she amended grimly.

The judge's housekeeper, a woman in her late thirties, still pretty, still with so much life ahead of her, had died instantly, according to the coroner's preliminary findings. And, despite the fact that the hit-and-run had occurred on the corner of a well-traveled street, there had been no witnesses to see what had happened. At least none who had come forward so far.

But it was still early.

Because there were no witnesses, there would have been no reason to suspect that the dead woman, who had been in the judge's employ for just over four years, hadn't been alone.

If it wasn't for the pink backpack found twenty feet from the body.

Rachel Montgomery's backpack.

A backpack but no Rachel Montgomery.

And it was up to her to tell this to the judge. To tell him that the peaceful world he'd left just a short while ago was no more. His housekeeper was gone and quite possibly so was his daughter.

Staring at the black door closest to her, Callie squared her shoulders. This kind of thing was never easy. Adams had said he was willing to go see the judge and tell him what had happened, but she'd vetoed that. He'd looked at her in surprise when she had volunteered to be the one to break the news to Montgomery. But there was a reason for that.

She knew the judge. Once upon a time, they'd had a brief connection. Before life with all its details had gotten in the way.

Into the valley of death rode the 600, she thought as she pushed open the door. Her path was immediately blocked by a tall man in dark livery. He looked like a solid wall of muscle and he wasn't about to go anywhere.

"Can't go in there," the bailiff warned. "Court's in session." He motioned for her to remove herself voluntarily. Or he would do it for her.

In her head Callie was aware of some giant timepiece, ticking the minutes away. Ticking away the minutes of Rachel Montgomery's life.

She had her identification out in less time than it took to think about it. Callie held it up to the bailiff, who stared at it with a note of skepticism in his eyes.

"I realize it's in session," she said as patiently as she could, "but Judge Montgomery is going to want to hear this."

Still the man was not about to go anywhere. Or let her go, either. "Tell me, Detective. I'll tell him."

"It's about his housekeeper. And his daughter," she added, unwilling to reveal anything further. If she'd wanted a third party to take care of this, she would have phoned the courthouse and brutally left a message.

Just as she uttered the word *daughter,* Brent raised his penetrating blue eyes away from the face of the youthful offender before him and looked toward the back of the room.

Right at her.

Chapter 2

He knew her.

Brent looked at the woman in the light-gray suit who'd just walked into his courtroom. Recognition set in instantly. In the space of one extraordinary moment, the entire scenario returned to him in total. From beginning to end.

He'd been at a charity fund-raiser, one of those boring things he was obligated to attend. He hadn't been appointed a judge yet, but there were whispers, rumors. And he knew he couldn't displease the gods in charge even though he would much rather have been home, dressed in his oldest clothes, standing over his daughter's crib, watching her breathe.

It seemed like little enough to ask, to stand in awe and watch a miracle breathe.

Besides, he and Jennifer were riding the cusp of

another one of their eternal disagreements and he hadn't felt like putting on his public face, the one that appeared unperturbed by anything. He hated glad-handing, hated being anything but genuine.

But there was the pending judgeship to consider, and Jennifer would have given him no peace if he'd declined the invitation to the event. So he'd accepted and made the best of it. Making small talk with even smaller people.

His wife was off somewhere in the huge ballroom, politicking. Rubbing elbows and who-knew-what-else with men she thought might further her life and his career. Or maybe just her life.

He remembered feeling completely cut off from everyone and everything, and longing just to go home.

And then he'd seen *her.*

Surrounded by men who bore vague resemblances to her, leaving him to guess, to hope, that they might be family rather than ardent admirers. As if that could possibly matter to him in his position. He was hopelessly married.

That had been the word for it. *Hopelessly.* Because there seemed to be little hope that his marriage could transform into what he'd first thought it might become. Happy. Fulfilling. Tranquilizing.

A surge of all three feelings, plus a host of a great many more shot through him the first time he looked in her direction. In the direction of the most exquisite creature he'd ever seen.

Her hair wasn't pulled back the way it was now,

in a thick braid the color of wheat the instant it first ripened. It had been loose about her bare shoulders then, sweeping along them with every movement she made. Creating havoc in his gut as he found himself wanting to do the same with his fingers.

She was wearing something light and gauzy and blue. It seemed to be held against her body by magic. Certainly not gravity, which should have been on his side and sent the garment pooling down to her strappy, high-heeled sandals.

He remembered there was music. The first he'd become aware of that night, even though the band had been playing all evening and would continue to do so for the remainder of the event.

He wasn't quite sure how he came to find himself standing in front of her, or where he unearthed the courage to introduce himself to her. He didn't normally do things like that. He was given to hanging back and observing. It was both his failing and his strength. Standing on the perimeter of life where he felt he could do the most good. Impartially.

Maybe he'd come forward because he recognized the man standing to the woman's left. Andrew Cavanaugh, the retired police chief of Aurora. Her father, he was to learn later. The others were her brothers and cousins.

Whatever the reason that had prompted him to shed his cloak of silence, he was suddenly standing before her. Introducing himself and asking her if she would like to dance. Something else he didn't do willingly, even though he'd been instructed in the

fine art of dancing only recently. Jennifer had insisted on it. So he wouldn't embarrass her, she'd
said.

He had no desire to embarrass Jennifer. Had no
thoughts of his wife whatsoever. For the space of a
score of heartbeats, she was completely excised from
his brain, if not his life.

He vividly remembered the way Callie Cavanaugh's smile had gone straight to his head as she'd
raised her eyes to his and accepted the hand he held
out. Remembered how low her voice was, like fine,
hundred-year-old brandy being reverently poured
into a crystal glass. Low and sexy.

Remembered, too, the electricity, the tension, the
indescribable feeling of lightness that came over him
as he held her in his arms and danced.

One small dance, a simple exchange of words, and
a connection was made that felt as if it had been
forged out of steel in the beginning of time.

Before.

He'd looked down into her eyes and gotten lost.

But he had a child and a position and a wife—
who intruded into the moment the instant the music
faded away. Like an avenging hawk, jealous that her
cast-off had attracted someone else's attention, Jennifer had swooped down from wherever it was that
she had been roosting to reclaim what was hers.

And he was obliged to let her.

Even though his eyes followed Callie as she
moved from the floor.

He had no idea what they called it. A connection,

chemistry, kismet. Some term invented by inert poets who had nothing better to do than to bury people in rhetoric. He couldn't put a label to it himself. All he knew was that he'd felt something nameless. Something wonderful. Something he'd never felt before. Or since. Something that whispered into his ear ''If only'' long after the dance, the fund-raiser itself, was over.

If only...

But the timing then had been all wrong.

As it was now.

Brent roused himself, realizing that he'd paused and that his secretary and his aide were both unabashedly staring at him.

''Court is in session.'' He shot an accusing look at the bailiff in the rear of the room. The latter raised his hands helplessly.

Callie circumvented the man, her attention on Brent. God, but he had only gotten better looking since she'd seen him. The next moment, she upbraided herself. How could she even think something like that? She was here to give him awful news, not appraise his appearance.

''Excuse me, Your Honor.'' She took another step toward him, only to find herself in a dance now with the bailiff who tried to get in front of her. ''I need a word with you.''

Brent hated disruptions. ''Can't it wait, Officer Cavanaugh?''

''Detective Cavanaugh,'' Callie automatically corrected, wishing what she had to say could be put off. "And no, I'm afraid it really can't."

Brent looked to his left, to his aide, Edwin Cambridge, who in turn looked pained as he stared down at the calendar he had drawn himself to accommodate the judge's cases. Precision was Edwin's passion. He felt it a matter of honor to have things running smoothly in the court.

The man sighed, then gave a small, almost imperceptible nod of his head.

"There'll be a slight recess," Brent announced to the two opposing lawyers, who looked at him with exasperation. The plaintiff was seated to the far left of the center. The man, barely in his twenties, looked greatly relieved at the interruption, like someone who had been granted a stay from the governor just before the switch was thrown.

Brent beckoned Callie forward. He wondered if she'd ever married that detective he'd heard she was engaged to and what had brought her into his courtroom today. Had there been a bomb threat? Should they be evacuating? After the events that had rocked the country very recently, nothing seemed impossible anymore.

"Make this quick, Detective Cavanaugh," he demanded, suppressing the urge to ask her how she'd been since that evening. "I have a very full schedule today."

"You have a full schedule every day," Edwin informed him.

Brent chose to ignore the man. It seemed simpler

that way than to engage in a dialogue with him. Edwin liked getting in the last word.

"You might want to reschedule your cases," Callie suggested tactfully as she followed Brent to his chambers.

Brent closed the door behind her, locking Edwin out, much to the latter's displeasure, then turned around. The judge crossed his arms, looking for all the world like an angel of darkness to her.

"All right, Detective, I'm waiting. And this had better be good," he warned her, although a part of him didn't believe that she would just waltz into his courtroom without a damn good reason.

Callie took a breath. "Actually, it's not. It's bad." Her eyes met his. There was no easy way to do this, no way to prepare someone for the words she was about to say. There wasn't even a way to prepare herself to say them. They felt like molten lead in her mouth, and even while she wanted nothing more than to expel them, she knew the damage they would do the second they were out. "Very bad."

Something seized his gut, tightening it so that for a moment he stopped breathing. A prayer materialized out of nowhere as he hoped that, for whatever reason, the woman he'd once held in his arms and danced with was overstating the matter.

"I didn't realize that you have a flare for the dramatic."

If only. If only this wasn't more than she thought it was and the little girl was somewhere, safe but frightened, hiding. Ready to be found.

Callie pressed her lips together, wishing it was so. But the truth was all she'd ever known and she couldn't sugarcoat this. "I don't."

The two words hung in the air between them, foreboding. Frightening.

He tried not to let his imagination run away with him. It couldn't be helped.

Was this about his wife?

His ex-wife, Brent amended. The first in his family to don black robes and become a judge, he was also the first in his family to get a divorce. Not all firsts were commendable, he'd thought bitterly at the time. Just unavoidable. Had this woman come to tell him that something had happened to Jennifer?

Inner instincts had him bracing himself. "Well then, what is it, Detective? I really—"

Do it. It's like ripping off a Band-Aid. The faster, the better.

Her father had counseled her with that. She was not entirely sure if that was the best approach to use. All she knew was that she didn't want to prolong this any more than was absolutely necessary.

Sympathy flooded through her as she said, "Your housekeeper was killed this morning."

Brent stared at her as if she'd just spoken in tongues. He'd just seen his housekeeper, what, two, two and a half hours ago. How could she possibly be dead?

"Delia? Killed?" he echoed in blatant disbelief. "How?"

Beneath the composure she could see that he was

genuinely upset. Was it just shock? Or was there something more going on between the judge and the crumpled woman who had been reduced to a chalk outline by the cruel whimsy of fate?

"Hit-and-run."

The words were only marginally sinking in. And then fear sprang up, huge and hoary, seizing him by the throat.

Rachel.

"What time?"

Callie blinked, thinking she'd misheard the question. "Excuse me?"

"What time?" he demanded again, his voice rising, booming about the small chambers. "What time was she killed?"

Callie thought back to the coroner's estimation. "Approximately eight o'clock."

Approximately. Delia always liked to be early. Had the housekeeper gotten his daughter to school before eight and been on her way home when the car had struck her?

Or—

His mind couldn't, *wouldn't* go there. Not if it didn't have to.

As if he were poised on a spring, Brent suddenly turned from the woman in his room and began dialing the phone on his desk. Halfway through, he realized he'd transposed two of the numbers. Swallowing a curse, telling himself that everything, at least for Rachel, was all right, he began dialing again.

"Judge, who are you—"

Callie didn't get a chance to finish her question, to ask the judge who he was calling. The expression on his face as he looked up at her stopped her dead, sucking out her very breath.

There was controlled terror in his eyes.

"She was taking my daughter to school. I want to find out if Rachel is in her classroom."

Very gently Callie placed her hand over his to stop him. The man needed more information before he called anyone. He deserved it.

Callie hated this, absolutely hated this. But he had to be told. "We found your daughter's backpack at the scene."

Brent could feel the blood draining out of his face as he looked at the woman who was discharging the nail gun straight at his heart.

"Where is she?" Everything inside of him was shaking, and it was all he could do not to allow it to take complete control.

Was he going to go into shock? She looked toward the chair behind him. Maybe she could get him to sit down. "Your Honor—"

He felt like shaking her, grabbing her waist and squeezing out of her the words he needed to hear. Why was she putting him through this? Why this torture in slow motion?

"Where is she?" he demanded again, his voice bouncing along the walls of the small, austere chambers like captive thunder.

Callie hated this feeling of helplessness. She knew everything took time, that good police work was far removed from magic or the quick solutions that the public was spoon-fed via TV dramas. But that didn't keep her from wishing she had answers for this heart-broken father standing before her.

She curbed the urge to place a comforting hand on his shoulder, knowing it wouldn't be appreciated. Knowing he'd push it away.

"We don't know," she told him honestly. "We think she might have run off when she saw your housekeeper struck by the vehicle."

Brent shut his eyes, searching for strength, for resolve. He shook his head. "She wouldn't do that."

But even as he said the words, his brain demanded: *How do you know? How do you know what a traumatized five-year-old would do?* He knew he was operating on hope and nothing more.

Get hold of yourself, man. She's fine. She probably ran off to school. It's Delia who you should be concerned about.

Brent thought of the bright young woman who'd formed such a bond with his daughter. Delia had come to him with excellent references and a real hunger to make a difference in someone's life. Rachel had been that someone.

Still, denial was part of survival and it was strong. He looked at Callie, a kernel of hope popping up. Maybe there was some mistake. "Are you sure it was my housekeeper?"

She knew what he was asking, what he was hoping. Her heart went out to him. He hadn't had an easy time of it, and she admired the fact that he was

a single father. Like her father had been for the past
fifteen years.

Grimly, Callie took out the plastic-encased wallet
that the CSI agent had inserted into a bag at her
request and given to her. Delia Culhane's wallet had
been placed inside, opened to the woman's driver's
license. Callie held it up for the judge's benefit.

"Oh, God." He took it into his hands, staring at
the woman's face through the plastic. The license
hardly did her justice. It didn't capture the sparkling
eyes, the laughter that his daughter was so quick to
respond to. "Did she suffer?"

Callie continued to watch every nuance that passed
over the judge's face. She felt like a voyeur and
hated it, but this was her job. To read people and
look for telltale signs that gave them away. She
didn't have to like it.

"Coroner said she died instantly."

At least that was something. Brent nodded, hand-
ing the bagged wallet back to her, his eyes on the
telephone on his desk. He was dialing again the moment Callie took the wallet from him.

Callie tucked the wallet back into the wide pockets
of her jacket. She indicated the telephone. "Are you
calling your daughter's school?"

He nodded, then raised his eyes to hers. Maybe
she was right. Maybe Rachel had run off, hurrying
to the school to notify someone about what had happened. She was a bright little girl, a feisty girl, far
older than her young years. Rachel would know that

Delia would need help. He pressed the last button on the keypad.

"It's all I can think of."

It was a logical next move. "Where does she—"

He heard the question begin, but his attention suddenly shifted to the voice that was coming from the other end of the receiver. A high, sweet voice that was asking him how she might direct his call.

"Principal Walsh, please." He struggled to sound calm. "Yes, this is an emergency."

Brent shut his eyes as a click and then silence greeted him. The operator had placed him on hold. Placed his very life on hold.

He felt a hand touch his black-draped arm.

He was still wearing his judge's robe, he realized. Somehow that struck him as ironic, given the fact that at this moment he felt as if there was no justice in the world. Not if hardworking women could be struck down and left like so much litter on the road. Not when young children, babies really, could vanish on their way to school in a city where they were supposed to be safe.

The detective was looking at him, compassion in her blue-gray eyes.

"If you give me the name of the school, I can have someone there probably before you get taken off hold," Callie told him helpfully.

He was about to tell her the school's name when he heard a click and then a woman's deep voice echoing in his ear. It was the school's principal. The one time he'd met her, he remembered thinking she looked like a feminine version of a U.S. Marines drill sergeant. He also remembered thinking that Rachel would be safe in a place run by a woman like that.

"Yes, this is Judge Brenton Montgomery. My daughter attends the morning kindergarten sessions at your school. Could you have someone check to see if she arrived this morning? Rachel Montgomery," he said in reply to the question. "No, I don't remember her teacher's name." He almost lost his patience, then fought to regain it. "No, wait, it's Preston, Presley, something like that. Yes, Peterson, that's right. Mrs. Peterson. Could you please check if Rachel arrived? Because there's been an accident, that's why."

What a hollow phrase that was, he thought in disgust. There's been an accident. Delia Culhane's life was cut short and it could be explained away by a single sentence that consisted of four words. It just didn't seem right or fair.

He blew out a breath, the last of his patience tethered by a thin thread. "Yes, I'll hold."

Brent turned from the wall and looked at Callie. He felt as if he was tottering on the very brink of hell, waiting to plunge down into the fires below as he stood there listening to the sound of silence pulsing against his ear. Waiting until the principal's messenger returned and she in turn told him what he wanted to hear. That Rachel was miraculously there.

Or was that pulsing sound his own heart, marking time, waiting, hoping?

Praying.

But Bristol and Oak was such a huge intersection and Rachel was such a little girl. Would she have run across it, terrorized by the sight of her beloved nanny being hit by a car?

Or was she still somewhere in the area, hiding? Crying. Waiting for him to come and rescue her. He wanted to be down there, looking for her. His inertia was strangling him.

Placing a hand over the receiver's mouthpiece, he turned toward Callie.

"Was it a drunk driver?" What other explanation could there be for hitting someone? No matter that it was early, maybe someone was still celebrating something from the night before. And death had stolen in at the end of the celebration.

Her own negative answers wearied her. "We don't know. We don't have any real details yet."

"What did the witnesses say?"

"We haven't found any witnesses. Yet," she emphasized.

Of course they hadn't, he realized. If there were witnesses, someone would have been able to tell them where his daughter was. Which direction she'd gone in. He wasn't thinking straight.

Callie saw Brent suddenly stiffen, his eyes intent as a voice came on the line. She didn't hear the words, only the muffled sound of someone talking.

She didn't need to hear the words. She read his expression.

The receiver slipped from Brent's fingers to the cradle beneath. Dread washed over him as he looked at Callie.

"Rachel didn't come to class today."

Chapter 3

Callie's heart immediately went out to him.

It wasn't the first time she'd seen that look of complete devastation; the look that said the person's insides had just been seized and twisted into a knot. Fifteen years ago she'd seen it on her own father's face.

For the sake of his children, Andrew Cavanaugh had kept up a good front the night his wife's car had been found nearly submerged in the river. So good a front that Callie had thought perhaps her parents' arguments had taken their toll and he'd ceased to care for her mother.

But then Callie had come up behind him late that second night, when the hopelessness of the situation had hit him and he'd thought he was alone. And heard him quietly crying.

It was a sound she would never forget. It marked the first time that her very secure world had been breached. The first time the door to that world had been thrown open, leaving them all vulnerable, and she realized that no one was ever completely safe.

Nothing had brought it home to her more acutely than when Kyle had been killed right in front of her eyes. Her fiancé hadn't even known that she had reached him a heartbeat later, that she'd held him to her on the sidewalk in front of the bank and sobbed his name over and over again. He was already dead by then. As dead as the man she had shot an instant before she'd reached Kyle. Shot and killed the bank robber who had first turned his weapon on her—the man who had killed Kyle.

Callie struggled to get her emotions under control now, struggled to keep a steady voice. Emotions only impeded progress on the cases she worked. She more than anyone else knew that.

She glanced toward the back of the framed photograph on Brent's desk. ''I'm going to need a recent photograph of your daughter, Judge. The sooner we have police officers looking for her, the sooner we'll find her.''

He nodded numbly, feeling like a man who was underwater and drowning. His brain seemed to be processing everything in slow motion. But he knew the credo. ''Every minute counts.''

''Yes, it does.'' She took out her pad, ready to jot down any shred of information that could be used. ''How much does she weigh?''

At first his mind was blank, then he remembered. Delia had told him the information after Rachel's last pediatric checkup. "Forty-eight, no, forty-nine pounds."

"Height?"

"Three foot three." He looked at her. "She's small for her age."

She offered him a smile she knew wasn't going to help, but she felt bound to try, anyway. "Do you remember what she was wearing this morning?"

He opened his mouth to tell her, but this time when no words came out, there was no belated memory to struggle to the foreground. "Something blue. I think." Damn it, why hadn't he looked at Rachel? "I didn't notice," he confessed.

Didn't notice because he was late. Because today was his day to preside over his court a half hour earlier because his docket was so overcrowded. So he hadn't looked at his daughter because he had to listen to some jaded lawyer plead the case of an equally jaded two-bit drug dealer. And because of these two people who mattered less than nothing to him, he hadn't sat down to breakfast with his daughter, hadn't noticed what she was wearing.

Hadn't kissed her goodbye.

The knot inside of him twisted a little more. He looked toward Callie as he upbraided himself. "I didn't kiss her goodbye."

Callie looked up from the note she'd just made. "Excuse me?"

Damn it, what was wrong with him? Rachel was

the most important person in his world, how could he have just ignored her like that? What kind of father *was* he?

Callie saw Brent square his shoulders like a man prepared to face a firing squad for his transgressions. "This morning when I left the house I was in a hurry. I didn't kiss Rachel goodbye. It was the first time I didn't kiss her goodbye."

As far as she was concerned, that placed him head and shoulders above a great many fathers she knew. "You'll kiss her twice to make up for it when we bring her back."

"When," he echoed. He wasn't the kind of man who deluded himself. He wasn't an optimist by nature. Yet he wanted to cling to the single word.

"When," Callie repeated firmly. As far as she was concerned, it was a promise. She couldn't operate any other way. Every crime was to be solved, every missing person to be found. The thought of failure was impossible at this juncture. "We're going to find your daughter, Judge. The success record for recovering children is getting better all the time."

"Better" meant that there were failures. But he already knew that.

No, he couldn't go there, couldn't allow himself to think that he might never see Rachel again, never sit at a table again, cheating at Old Maid for the pleasure of seeing her laugh with glee because she'd won again. She was the only bright light in his life, and he would have gladly given up his own life to ensure that she would be returned, unharmed.

"Judge, the photograph," Callie prodded gently, nodding toward the frame.

He took it from his desk and handed it to her. Callie quickly removed the photograph from its frame. She placed the empty frame on the desk, then looked at the photograph. It was a professional portrait, taken at a studio. Happiness radiated from the small face and intelligent eyes. She could almost hear the little girl giggling.

"I'll get this back to you as soon as possible," Callie promised.

She had nearly reached the door before the fact that she was leaving registered with Brent. He felt as if a vacuum had suddenly been created around him. He knew he couldn't just stay here.

"Wait." He threw off his robes, tossing the black garment in the general direction of his chair. "I'm coming with you."

She stopped dead. The sympathy she felt for him did not interfere with her duty. "You know the rules, Judge. You can't do that."

Yes he knew the rules, but he was in no-man's-land now and rules didn't work here, didn't mean anything. "I'm not the judge right now." Crossing to her, he looked down into her eyes. "I'm Rachel's father. I'm Brent."

She'd called him that once, he recalled. Long ago when they had danced. When Rachel had been safe.

He was making this hard for her, Callie thought. And though he'd just thrown the title aside, his being a judge might very well be the reason all this was happening. But it was still early and she didn't want to heap theories on the man until she had a few more facts to work with.

"I need you to go home," she told him as gently as possible. "There might be a ransom call."

Ransom. Money.

Bitterness rose up in his throat as he turned the words over in his head. Ever since he could remember, his wealth had always been more a burden than a joy. It had made him doubt who his friends were. Then he'd discovered that Jennifer had been far more attracted to his wealth and his potential prestige than she had been to him.

And now was money the reason his daughter had been snatched?

What other conclusion could there be? "Then you do think she's been kidnapped." It wasn't a question, it was a resigned statement.

Callie surprised him by shaking her head. "It's far too early in the game to make a call, Jud—Brent," she said. "But it's always wise to keep all the options open. I'm still hoping your daughter just ran off. She witnessed a traumatic scene this morning. Anyone would have run off."

Another shaft went through his heart. That Rachel had gone through something like that by herself, without having him there to shield her, broke his heart. Rachel was just a baby. Babies were supposed to feel secure, to know nothing but simple, happy times, not see someone they loved killed right before their eyes.

"She shouldn't have seen that."

Callie heard the accusation in his voice and in-
stinctively knew he was blaming himself. That
wasn't going to help either him or his daughter. "It's
a very hard world, Brent. We can't protect our children forever."

He looked at her. "You have children?"

"No. I was speaking figuratively." She had to get
going. Callie opened the door behind her. "Go home,
Brent. Someone will be there to talk with you
shortly—"

"You," Brent said firmly. He'd heard via the
grapevine that she was an outstanding detective, very
much a credit to her father and her family name. All
the Cavanaughs were. He wanted, *needed,* the best
right now. "I want you to be the one to come to the
house and tell me what's happening."

She was about to protest that she was going to be
out in the field, but then stopped herself. She could
stretch a minute here, borrow a quarter of an hour
there and somehow find the time. He deserved that
kind of consideration. Everyone going through what
he was going through did.

Besides, the most odious part of this investigation
was still ahead of them. Like it or not, she was going
to have to question Brent to make sure that he hadn't
choreographed his own daughter's abduction for
some macabre reason of his own. Of all the things
she had to do while working a missing child case,
she hated this part most of all. Hated pointing a
veiled finger at a parent while their heart was already

splintered in a thousand pieces over what might have happened to their child.

These were the rules, she reminded herself. If they were going to make any headway, she had to follow the rules. It was all any of them had. And in times of turmoil, rules were what held them together when everything around them demanded that they fall apart. Rules and order had been what had kept her going after Kyle had been taken from her. Following rules, keeping to a schedule.

Placing one foot in front of the other until somehow, paths from here to there were made.

She was still placing one foot in front of the other, Callie thought. But now she was a little more clear on where she was going. And the place beneath her feet felt a little more like solid ground, a little less like clouds.

She nodded in response to his request. Or maybe it wasn't so much of a request as a mandate. Not that she could blame him.

"I'll be there as soon as I can."

He looked at her. It would have to do. "Send in my aide on your way out, will you? He's probably right outside, trying to hear what's going on."

She nodded, offering him an encouraging smile as she left the chambers.

A little more than an hour later, Callie was driving up the long hill that led to Brent Montgomery's home. She'd left the photograph of the bright-eyed, smiling blond child with Greg Harris, the computer operative they had on loan from the PR division of the police department. Greg's instructions were to print several thousand copies of Rachel Montgomery's photograph, along with a short description as to her vitals and what was presumably her last known location. Bristol and Oak, where Delia Culhane had been struck down by the vehicle.

The intersection outside of the upscale development was a busy one. While Bristol itself wasn't Aurora's main thoroughfare, each end of it led onto a freeway. Someone had to have seen something, Callie argued with herself. They just had to get the word out as quickly as possible and hope that one of Aurora's good citizens stepped up. Fast.

This was definitely not a tract house, Callie thought as she pulled up the circular driveway. With its stone facade, the house where Brent and his daughter lived reminded her of a medieval castle. The place where she had grown up could have easily fit into the building twice.

Maybe two and a half times, she mused, getting out of her car. She couldn't begin to imagine what someone with just one child could do with all that space. It seemed cold and removed to her. Perfect for a museum. In her father's house, they were always tripping over each other, but somehow that seemed cozier.

Her heels clicked on the gray-and-white cobblestones as she hurried up the walk to the door.

The doorbell had hardly peeled once before the massive door was being opened. Brent was in the doorway, the tiny spark of hope in his eyes extinguishing the moment he looked at her face.

The structure should have dwarfed him, but it didn't. He seemed to be a perfect match for his surroundings. Powerful, commanding a feeling of awe and respect.

And massive sympathy, she thought, looking into his eyes. Dark blue, they seemed endlessly deep with pain. And she had nothing to tell him that would change that. Yet.

"The technicians will be coming soon," she told him as she entered.

"Technicians?"

"To wire the phones." A place like this had to have a battalion of telephones. She turned to look at him. "In case there is a ransom call." She could see what he was thinking, that the kidnapper would know to hang up before the call could be traced. "Not every criminal has a genius IQ. That only happens in the movies. Most kidnappers are greedy, and their greed causes them to slip up. When they do, we'll be right there." He closed the door behind her. For a moment the silence embraced her, bringing with it a huge sadness. She struggled against the urge to offer empty platitudes. "How are you holding up?"

He'd been raised to keep a stiff upper lip when it came to the public. There was to be no hint of scandal, no implication that everything wasn't perfect. He was a Montgomery, and perforce, everything *was* perfect. Or so the facade went. Inbred instincts brought the immediate response of "fine" to his lips, and then he paused. He took his responsibility as judge solemnly to heart. That meant he couldn't lie.

"I'm not."

She was surprised by his honesty. Most men pretended they could handle any situation that came their way, whether they could or not. That put in him a very small, rare class.

"This will all be in the past soon enough, Judge—Brent." She corrected herself again when she saw him look at her sharply. Belatedly she realized what he would read into her words.

"Did you find out anything?"

"Not yet." Guilt washed over Callie. She hadn't meant to mislead him, only to offer hope. "The CSI team on the scene is working on identifying the kind of car the man who killed your housekeeper was driving."

Most of the vehicles that frequented the road fell into four or five categories, popular models of economical foreign cars. "How's that going to help find my daughter?"

She knew how frustrating this had to be for him. They were crawling when he wanted to be running. "Every piece of the puzzle is necessary in order to create the total picture." She gave him something positive to work with. "In the meantime, we have beat cops going door to door with your daughter's photograph. If she's in the area, willingly or unwillingly," Callie emphasized, "we will find her."

She believed what she was saying, he thought. But he knew the odds. He couldn't have been a judge in the criminal system if he didn't. "And if she's not in the area?"

"We will still find her."

She looked around the immediate area. The foyer led into a spacious living room that seemed much larger for its restraint in furnishings. There were no antiques, no museum pieces gracing walls or tables. This was a house that belonged to a man who felt no need to prove anything to anyone. A man who was confident in his own skin. It would take a lot to rattle him. And he had been rattled. Badly. It was time to share her theories with him.

"You know, there is a chance that someone might have been stalking your housekeeper and that this was strictly about her. Did Ms. Culhane have any boyfriends, odd friends…?" Her voice trailed off, letting him fill in the blanks.

Brent took no time to think. He didn't have to. "Not that I know of."

The housekeeper wouldn't have been the first one to have a secret life her employer didn't know about. "What did she do on her days off?"

It was hard not to pace about the room. Brent could feel the pressure building up inside of him, searching for release.

"Stayed here most of the time. She really cared about Rachel." He wasn't giving the woman her due, he thought. In his concern about his daughter's safety, Delia had become a footnote. "Delia was a great help when Rachel's mother left. I don't know what I would have done if she hadn't been here."

She noticed the way he structured the sentence, referring to the woman as Rachel's mother rather than his wife or ex-wife. Jennifer Montgomery must have hurt him a great deal, Callie thought, for Brent to have iced over his heart this way.

"Were you and Ms. Culhane—close?"

"She didn't like being called Ms." His mouth curved slightly as he remembered the speech Delia had given him. "Thought that sounded too vague. She was unmarried by choice and she had no problem with the world knowing it." He could see the detective was still waiting for an answer to her question. "If by 'close' you mean did we sometimes have lengthy talks about what we thought was best for Rachel, yes." His eyes darkened slightly at what he knew was the implication. "If you mean anything else, no."

Callie pressed on. "You didn't take her out to dinner or—"

Brent cut her short. "Once each year for her birthday. With Rachel," he added, his voice stony, cold. "And there is no 'or,' Detective. Delia Culhane was my housekeeper and Rachel's nanny. And a very, very good woman." He took offense for the woman who could no longer speak for herself. "She doesn't deserve the kind of thoughts you're having."

"I'm not having any thoughts, Judge." Callie used his title deliberately, to drive home the point that she was being professional, nothing more, nothing less. "I'm doing my job. The more information I have, the better I can do it."

"Well, unless there's some deep, dark secret I didn't know about, my daughter's kidnapping," the term stung his tongue but he couldn't continue to pretend that it was anything else, "doesn't have anything to do with Delia beyond the obvious. That she died trying to protect my daughter."

Callie knew that was what he wanted to think, but she didn't have the luxury of allowing him to believe that without questioning the woman's integrity further. "Miss Culhane wouldn't have tried to take Rachel on her own, would she?"

He glared at her. "The woman is dead, Callie."

This was the first time he'd used her name, and she paused for a long moment to gather her thoughts.

Callie took a breath. "Yes, but maybe she orchestrated the kidnapping in order to get money—or revenge—" She still couldn't rule that out. Perhaps the woman felt she had received some slight or had some grievance against him. Even if it was imaginary, it still needed to be checked out. "And it backfired." There was no honor among thieves, there were only thieves. "Her partner decided that he couldn't share the money with her."

Brent was adamant as he shook his head. "She'd been with me since Rachel was a year old. Look, Callie, it's my job to read people. Delia Culhane didn't have a mean or mercenary bone in her body. She was entirely selfless."

Callie blew out a breath as she took in his information. Whether or not he was right still had to be determined, but for the moment she could pretend to believe him.

"All right, for the time being let's pretend that she was pure as the driven snow. Still, I need to look through her things, just as a formality." He wasn't fooled, she thought. "Would you mind showing me her room?"

With conscious effort he strove to take the edge off his temper. He knew she was just doing her job. "No, I wouldn't mind, but you're going entirely in the wrong direction." He looked at her. "Just as you will with your next tack."

God, but he was tall, she thought. And decidedly masculine. Even more than he'd been that night they danced. He seemed to draw the very air out of the room. "My next tack?"

This time he allowed himself the slightest hint of a smile. Because the very thought was hopelessly ludicrous. "Where you rule me out as a suspect."

He was going to make it easy for her. She was grateful for that. "Personally I don't see you as a suspect."

He wondered if she was patronizing him, then decided that she wasn't. Still he wanted his question answered. "And you're basing this on what? On our dancing together once?"

She hadn't expected him to oppose her on this, much less bring up that incident. She was equally surprised that he even remembered dancing with her. But she remembered.

Funny how some things just stuck in your mind.

She'd thought back to that evening, that dance, more than once. She couldn't even say why, because she had never allowed her thoughts free rein when it came to that memory. He'd been married and she wasn't the type to be with a married man in any way that wasn't completely public.

"On your reputation," she replied tersely. "And on the fact that you know my father. Dad's a damn good judge of character." She smiled at him. "And he always liked you."

He went at it like the lawyer he'd once been. "Hearsay."

"All right, then, on my gut instinct."

Again Brent overruled her. "Not admissible in court."

She looked at him. "You *want* me to question you like a suspect?"

He knew this had to be done and he wanted it over with as fast as possible. "I want you to rule me out as a suspect. Officially."

"All right, then." She took a deep breath and began asking him questions as they walked to the rear of the main floor and his late housekeeper's room.

Chapter 4

"I want my daddy. Where's my daddy?"

Rachel wiggled against the restraints that had been added to her seatbelt. It was like the time Tommy Edwards threw ropes around her when he was playing Spider-Man. He told her they were webs, but they weren't.

She could hardly move.

Outside the rear passenger window, scenery she'd never seen before whizzed by. She screwed her eyes shut tight for a second, determined not to cry. Crying was for babies, and she wasn't a baby. She was a big girl. Delia always told her so.

The thought of her nanny, lying on the road where cars could hit her if she didn't get up brought a tight, scratchy feeling to her throat, making it feel as if it was going to close up.

Rachel struggled against that, too. She had to be brave. Brave until her daddy came for her. She knew he would.

She wanted to have his arms around her now, making her feel safe. Why wasn't he coming?

Where *was* he?

Sucking in air, she looked through the closed window and screamed "Dad-dee!" as loud as she could. But there was no one to hear her anymore. There were no people here. Just her and this man who had grabbed her, pulling her into his funny-looking car.

Delia had tried to grab her back, screaming for help, but he'd pushed her away. And then, when she'd tried to pull open the door, he'd made the car spin around. There was a big "Whap" and she heard Delia scream once. When she'd struggled to look out the window, Delia was lying down. She'd tried to call to her, but the man had pulled her back, holding her by the arm and squeezing. Hard. Squeezing until she promised not to cry out.

She'd promised, but he'd held on to her anyway, driving with just one hand. He held her like that until they were someplace she'd never seen before. Then he'd tied her up and put her in the back seat.

She wanted her daddy.

He looked at her in his rearview mirror. She was a spunky little kid.

Like his Alice was.

The thought of his daughter brought a fresh salvo of pain to the middle of his chest, stoking the red-hot fire in his belly. He hadn't seen Alice in five years, didn't even have any idea where she was now. That bitch had taken her away, the one who had promised to stick by him. For richer, for poorer, in sickness and in health. Just not during a jail sentence.

He pressed his lips together, forcing his mind forward. He'd lost Alice. For now. But he'd found another. This was going to be his Alice now. The goddamned judge owed him that.

Hell, Montgomery owed him a lot more, but this would do. For starters.

"You can call for your daddy all you want," he told the little girl mildly. He took care to keep his voice low, nonthreatening. He didn't want to scare her. He wanted her happy. And to love him. Just like Alice had. "But it won't do you any good. He gave you to me. Said you were mine now."

Something funny was happening in her tummy. It felt like ants running up and down inside. Red-hot ants. She'd felt like this when she'd watched that movie on TV, the one about witches. Until Delia had turned it off.

Rachel began breathing hard, frightened. Telling herself that her daddy wouldn't do that to her. He'd never give her away. He loved her.

But he hadn't kissed her goodbye today. He'd left without even talking to her.

She could feel tears stinging the corners of her eyes and stuck out her lower lip. "That's not true."

He liked the fire he saw. She was like him, never

giving up. Good. "Yes, it is. He doesn't have time for you anymore. He's too busy being a judge."

Busy. Daddy said he was in a hurry this morning. And he'd left fast. "My daddy always has time for me," she declared, but she wasn't so sure anymore.

He raised his eyes to look at the small face in the rearview mirror. She was petulant. He was gaining, he thought, satisfied with himself. "He didn't even kiss you goodbye this morning, did he?"

It hadn't been a difficult matter for him to break into the house yesterday, when the housekeeper had gone to pick the little girl up, and plant two cameras in the house, one in the living room, one in the kitchen. Child's play for a man of his talents, really. And he had seen everything.

The judge should have let him make restitution. Should have let him slide. Winked and looked the other way as a deal was struck. Not stripped him of everything. Not stolen his life.

Rachel's mouth fell open, and she stared at the back of the man's head. "How did you know that?"

A smile slid over his lips. He turned to look at the little girl in the back seat. There was no traffic here, no other cars at all. They were in the country now. And entirely on his terms.

"Easy. I'm an angel." Alice always liked angels. Had insisted on having them all over her room. On the wallpaper; scattered throughout her room. There'd been stuffed cherubs lining her shelves. She even wore one around her neck on a chain. He'd always called her his special angel. "Angels know everything."

Rachel bunched up her face, glaring at him contemptuously. "You're lying," she accused righteously. "You're not an angel. Angels don't drive cars."

He saw no reason to argue over this. She was too smart to be taken in. Probably didn't believe in Santa Claus, either. Good, that made things easier.

"No, you're right," he agreed, turning around again. "I'm not an angel. But I am your new daddy. So you'd better get used to the idea."

He flipped on the radio after fumbling with the controls for a moment.

Rachel screwed her eyes shut again. But this time as her lower lip quivered, a tear leaked out from beneath her lashes.

Brent paced back and forth in his den, his cordless phone against his ear. He was too upset, too restless to even attempt to sit down. "That's right, Carmella," he told the secretary on the other end of the connection, "a leave of absence. I'm taking a leave of absence."

"But, Judge, your calendar's full." The rustle of pages could be heard, mingling with the young woman's protest. He knew his schedule was never far from her reach.

Brent could hear how flabbergasted she was. Since they'd begun working together, he hadn't taken more than a few days off, all one at a time, weaving his life around his career the best way possible.

But this was different. This took precedence over everything else.

"Yes, I know, but it can't be helped." He rubbed his forehead, trying to think. The headache was getting the better of him, knocking thoughts into the background. "Judge Holstein always said he would cover for me if I needed it." It was time to call in favors. "And there's Judge Reynolds and Judge Wojohowitz. They can be counted on to pick up some of the slack."

Carmella sighed into his ear. He knew what she was thinking. Rescheduling the docket was going to be a severe challenge. She was good, but she wasn't a miracle worker. But that was exactly what he was in the market for right now, a miracle worker.

He wondered just how closely Callie Cavanaugh fit that description.

There was more shuffling of pages as she asked, "How long is this leave for?"

He couldn't tell her that it was open-ended. For one thing, her protest would be heated, for another, that meant admitting to himself that his daughter wasn't going to be found by the end of the day.

Or two.

For once in his life Brent forced himself to be and sound optimistic.

"A week." He paused, and then, because he was what he was and optimism came at a high premium, he added, "And after that we'll see."

There was another pause on the line. Carmella was having trouble comprehending, he thought. A few days was reasonable, a week was stretching it. Since this was unexpected, fathoming anything else was close to impossible.

"Judge—"

He didn't want to hear it, didn't want to remain on the line with her anymore, even though Carmella Petrocelli was one of the most pleasant people he'd ever met and competent on top of that. The woman was dependability itself. He didn't want her asking questions. Carmella was one of those people who cared, and he couldn't handle that right now. It would make him break down.

"Do what you can, Carmella."

Like the small terrier she had as a pet, Carmella hung on. "Judge, does this have to do with that police detective this morning? Is anything wrong?"

Natural instincts had him wanting to say no, that everything was fine, but the news would be out soon enough. He tried to convince himself that this was for Rachel's good. The more people who actually knew, the better. It was just that it was so hard for him to admit that he was not in control of a situation and this time, he was so out of control it scared the hell out of him.

"My daughter's—" What could he say? Missing? No, she was more than missing, she was stolen. No amount of denial was going to change that. He began again, his mouth dry, the words sticking to the roof like bits of white, dampened bread. "My daughter's been kidnapped, Carmella."

"Oh, my God, Judge." The receiver echoed with her concern. "I...I don't know what to say. Is there anything I can do?"

Yes, find my daughter. Show me the bastard who did this so I can kill him for ever touching my little girl.

Brent had no idea how he managed it, after the admission he'd just made, but he kept his voice calm. "I'll let you know."

"I'll call the other judges right away," the woman promised. "And please, let me know the moment there's news. I'll pray for her."

"Thank you."

Brent hung up. His secretary's promise meant nothing to him. Prayer. What good was that? He couldn't pray, couldn't take solace in thinking a merciful God was listening. A merciful God wouldn't have allowed Rachel to be taken in the first place. Wouldn't have looked the other way while Delia's life had been snuffed out like a candle.

The study echoed an all pervasive silence.

God, but he missed her. Unless it was late at night, even with the door to his study closed he could always hear Rachel. Her laughter would snake through the vents and find its way to him. He'd taken that for granted. It was one of those small joys of life that you didn't realize was there until it no longer was.

He couldn't stay here, he decided abruptly. Couldn't just mark time, waiting for the phone to ring, for some kind of word to trickle down to him. If he stayed here like this any longer, he was going to go crazy.

Brent reached for the telephone again.

Callie blew out a breath as she sank down at her desk. She was tired, but at least something had been accomplished. The nanny had checked out. If Delia Culhane had a life beyond taking care of the Montgomery child and house, it was better hidden than that of a double agent's.

The past few hours had been spent talking to the teachers at Rachel's school, to Rachel's pediatrician and to the woman who ran the ballet classes that Rachel attended twice a week without fail. Everyone had nothing but glowing words to say about the woman who, until this morning, had taken care of her. Delia Culhane had no vices, no bad habits, apparently no outside friends. Her only hobby seemed to be watching musicals. There was a full library of old MGM musicals, both videotapes and audio CDs in her room.

Callie had one of the people on the task force get her a record of all out-going and in-coming calls from the Montgomery residence for the past three months. Every one checked out. Nothing unusual. A couple dozen calls to or from the courthouse, a few calls from what she surmised were Rachel's friends and one call to the pediatrician.

It didn't appear that the judge had much of a social life, either, unless he conducted all his calls by cell phone. She was going to have to remember to get those records, as well.

Callie frowned, making a notation to herself in her well-worn notepad.

This pretty much did away with the nanny connection. Eliminating Delia meant that the woman's death had been an accident. The nanny was probably killed trying to protect Rachel, possibly running after the vehicle when the driver had suddenly surprised Delia by turning the car around and aiming it at her.

Which meant they were dealing with someone who was cold-blooded and calculating. And he had the little girl. The task force was getting a list of all the known pedophiles in the area and bringing them in for questioning, but she didn't want to entertain that possibility, not yet. Despite herself and all her police training and background, Callie shivered.

"It's not cold in here."

She looked up and saw that Brent was approaching her desk. She'd only left him a few hours ago, but he'd become more gaunt, more haunted in that space of time. Not that either looked bad on him.

His ex-wife was an idiot, giving him up. The thought came to her out of nowhere.

Maybe it hadn't been the woman's choice, Callie thought.

She closed her notepad, sticking it back into her right front pocket. "What are you doing here?"

He'd seen her shiver and his thoughts had immediately flown to Rachel. Was that a reaction to something Callie had learned about his daughter? But she would have said something, he was certain. He'd heard that Callie was like her father, she didn't go in for drama or playing things out for attention. She was honest. That meant not keeping things back.

He held his hands in a gesture of servitude. "I'm here to help."

They'd already gone through this. She knew how he felt, but she couldn't have him just hanging around, getting in the way. "You can do that by staying home by the telephone in case there's a ransom call."

He didn't want her treating him as if he was some kind of novice, as if he didn't know how this went. They were both familiar with procedure. "It's been almost seven hours since Delia was killed and Rachel went missing. Since Rachel was abducted," he corrected. "There's been no call. The kidnapper usually calls to start things moving once the discovery is made."

He was right, but there were always exceptions. "Maybe this one doesn't have a handbook." She rose from her desk, ready to gently prod the man toward the door. "The only pattern you can count on is that there is no pattern."

He looked at her, wondering if she was patronizing him or giving him her philosophy. "You don't believe in profiling?"

"I believe in the unpredictable, Your Honor." Callie took his arm. The look he gave her was one of authority, meant to freeze her in her tracks. There was never any confusion who was in charge in his courtroom. But they weren't in his courtroom. They were on her turf and she got to make the calls. "Now, if you don't mind, Judge, I really have to get back to work."

With one precise gesture, Brent moved his elbow out of her range. He wasn't about to be ushered out the door like some guest who had overstayed his welcome.

"I have my sister and brother-in-law staying at the house just in case something falls through the cracks." He held up his cell phone for her benefit. "All my calls are being rerouted to my cell."

They'd bugged the telephones in his house, but not this one. If the call was rerouted, they'd miss their opportunity to hopefully trace it back to its source. She reached for the cell.

"We'll have to put a device in your cell—"

Her fingers brushed against his before he pulled the cell phone back and deposited it into his pocket. He had an ancestor who came from the old country, Brianne MacKenzie. Her village had thought of her as a witch. Legend had it they'd almost burned her at the stake before her future husband had whisked her away. She had what they called "The gift." She was a seer. Touching someone at times allowed her to make a connection, to see into that person's future or see something about them in a hazy flash.

Something seemed to crackle between them as Callie's fingers brushed against his, and he thought of his great-great-great-grandmother, wishing he had her abilities, just for a moment. So he could unlock doors closed to him.

He was looking at her oddly, Callie thought, as if he was trying to discern something about her. Or maybe he was just lost in thought. She couldn't blame him for being preoccupied.

"Brent?"

He shook himself free of the haze. "Already taken care of." His hand curled around the outline of the cell phone in his pocket. "I asked the technician who bugged the phones at the house to do it before he left."

Well, one problem down, a million to go. "Thinking ahead." She nodded her approval. A lot of people in this situation couldn't think at all.

His frown went down to the bone. "Not nearly fast enough."

Callie could read his mind. "It's not your fault she was taken."

She was trying her best to be kind, he thought. But this wasn't a time for kindness, it was a time for brutal honesty. If he were a bricklayer, his daughter would be home right now, trying to finish the simple homework the teacher had given the class so that she could sit and watch her favorite cartoons.

"It is if it's someone who's trying to get back at me," he replied grimly.

He was right, and there wasn't anything she could say to the contrary. Frustrated for him, Callie dragged her hand through the top of her hair.

"All right, since you're here, why don't we get

the rest of the questions out of the way?'' She gestured toward the chair on the other side of her desk and sat down in her own.

"Questions?'' They weren't going anywhere. After a beat, Brent sat down.

Callie pulled out a pristine white legal pad and placed it in the center of her desk. She tried to make this sound as innocuous as possible. Was there such a thing as an innocuous interrogation? She didn't think so. "About you, your relationship with your daughter, your ex-wife—''

His dark eyebrows drew together over his almost-perfect nose. He'd already tried to call his ex to tell her, but in typical Jennifer fashion, she was unreachable. "Jennifer? What does Jennifer have to do with it?''

"Maybe nothing, maybe everything.''

A couple of people came into the squad room. This was all wrong, she decided. She couldn't expect the judge to talk to her where almost anyone could overhear them. She looked around. Her captain's office was free. As far as she knew, the man was going to be out for the rest of the day. Something about a photo opportunity. The captain was always at his best when there was a supply of videotape around.

She rose again, taking her legal pad with her. She pointed out the glass-enclosed room. "Why don't we go into that office and talk?''

Did she think he needed privacy? That there was some kind of confession forthcoming? She was going to be sorely disappointed if she was leaning toward that. Brent held his ground. "We can talk out here, I have nothing to hide."

Maybe yes, maybe no. Privacy encouraged talking. "Good. But I like tight, secure places. Humor me," she requested. With that, she led the way to the captain's office.

With a pastel blue back wall, the office had three sides of glass. Or three walls buffered with blinds, depending on how you viewed it. Callie lowered all three blinds and closed them before she turned to talk to Brent. She made herself as comfortable as possible in the captain's chair. It was one of those ergonomic ones designed to relax your back. It always had the opposite effect on her, making her feel as if she was on a rack.

But this wasn't about her.

"Since you brought up your ex-wife," she began mildly, as if they were having a conversation over afternoon coffee, "let's talk about her."

He didn't need to be a seer like his ancestor to know where she was going with this. "You couldn't be more wrong."

Maybe he was a little too quick to judge, she mused. You never wanted to think the worst of someone you loved. Or loved once.

Callie phrased her words tactfully, not wanting to add unnecessarily to his pain. "Sometimes we don't know people as well as we think we do."

Brent held his position. He would have bet his life on this, and he wasn't the type to bet on anything except a sure thing. "Jennifer never wanted to be a mother. Rachel was an accident. One of those tiny percentages that manage to screw up the birth control industry's batting average. When Jennifer got pregnant, I had to talk her into keeping the baby. Having Rachel cost me the price of a full-length mink coat. Best return on an investment I ever had.''

So the woman also believed in murdering animals for their pelts. She knew she wasn't supposed to have an opinion of the judge's ex, but Callie was getting to like her less and less by the moment. Especially since Jennifer Montgomery apparently had no mothering instincts. Families were such a way of life in her world, she couldn't fathom someone not wanting a child.

She looked down at her pad. It was still snow-white, but she couldn't very well write "Ex-wife is a bitch.'' At least, not while the judge could read the words upside down. She folded her hands over the pad and looked at the man. "So she wouldn't suddenly try to have your daughter kidnapped?''

His laugh was short and without mirth. "It's all I can do to get Jennifer to visit Rachel a few times a year.'' Brent hated the way Rachel looked whenever Jennifer canceled a visit. He knew his daughter was trying to keep up a brave front for him, but he also knew that her feelings were deeply hurt. For that alone, he damned Jennifer. "Believe me, she has no interest in taking Rachel.''

Love wasn't always a motive. But oftentimes hate was. "Even to get back at you for something?''

Jennifer would have been more inclined to feel

that way if he hadn't allowed her out of their marriage. "The only thing my ex-wife wanted from me
was my last name and my money. She got a share
of both in the divorce. She also wanted to be free.
She couldn't wait to be rid of both of us. There is
no way that she would do anything like this."

This time she did write. "Ex-wife wants no part
of child." She looked up at Brent. "All right, if it's
not about your housekeeper and it's not about your
ex-wife, there are still two ways to go here. Someone
is trying to get revenge against you, or—" and this
was a very big or "—someone wanted to kidnap
your daughter." She had a feeling Brent already
knew this, but she made it a point to lay out the
foundations for every parent whose child had been
kidnapped. "Other than parental snatchings, kidnap-
pings occur for four reasons. To get a ransom, to
replace a lost child, real or imaginary," she tacked
on, knowing that one was just as strong a reason as
the other, "to sell the child, although those are usually younger than your daughter."

"That's three."

Was he asking her about the fourth? Or did he just
want it out of the way? "The fourth is for reasons
of pedophilia." But even as she stated it, she ruled
it out. At least, for now. "This was too awkward,
too difficult to be a random snatching by a pervert
who just happened to see your daughter and had
something triggered inside of him. That would have
been more likely had he been driving by your house

or walking by the schoolyard and seen her playing outside.''

He wanted to believe that, to believe that his child wasn't in any more danger than her kidnapping already placed her in. ''What do your instincts tell you?''

''Since there haven't been any ransom phone calls, I'm inclined to agree that this isn't about money. I'm more inclined than ever to think that this might be about revenge. Which brings us back to you.'' She looked at him pointedly. ''Has anyone threatened you in the past year or so, Brent?''

Threats were part of the territory. He could still remember how unsettled the first one had made him. It was only after three that he began to shrug them off. Until now.

''I've been a criminal court judge for five years, Callie. It would be unusual for me not to have been threatened.''

''All right, anyone in particular stand out in your mind?'' Before he could answer, she quickly added, ''This isn't to say that it might not be someone who has just quietly plotted revenge, but odds are, the vocal ones are more likely to carry out a threat.''

But why drag his daughter into this? ''Wouldn't a threat mean they'd tried to kill me?''

She could see he was struggling to suppress rage. ''You kill someone, it's over. Taking your daughter promises the kidnapper that you will be suffering for a very long, long time.''

He hated admitting it, but she was right. Brent

shook his head, hoping he would be able to get five minutes alone with the kidnapper. Even just three. "You have a very logical mind, Callie."

She blew out a breath. At times she was too logical. If she hadn't been so, she and Kyle would have been married; then they couldn't have been on the same squad and he wouldn't have taken that bullet meant for her.

"Yeah," she agreed quietly, "it's a curse."

Chapter 5

Brent's chambers at the courthouse seemed somehow more somber than they had before, as if the weight of what he was enduring had permeated his surroundings. Working with the vibrations coming off the man, Callie felt as if the very walls of the room had darkened and were closing in.

Without waiting to ask, Callie walked over to the curtained bay window behind Brent's desk and drew back the drapes. The late-afternoon sun immediately brightened the room tenfold.

Brent held his hand up before his eyes. In his present frame of mind, he felt the room had far too much light in it. "What are you doing?"

She moved away from the window. There were filing cabinets all along the adjacent wall. Oak, to match his desk. No one had to tell her that he had brought in his own cabinets. Standard issue was gun-metal gray, emphasis on the metal.

She wondered if they were for show, or if they were filled. "You need light."

He had thrown the light switch on when they'd walked in. "That's why they invented electricity."

Callie deliberately stood in front of the drawstrings on the drapes, blocking his access. "We'll use that, too, but nothing beats sunlight when it comes to il-luminating and to buoying up."

He frowned at her. The last thing he wanted was a cheerleader. He wouldn't have said she was the type. But his judgment wasn't exactly on target right now. "Do I look as if I want to be buoyed up?"

"No, but you need it." Her voice was noncon-frontational, but firm just the same. He had the feel-ing that she was accustomed to taking charge. "You can't give up hope. All we have is our faith and our hope to see us through."

There was that word again, *hope*, both his enemy and his friend. "I'm not giving up hope, I just don't believe in using crutches."

Her eyes held his for a long moment. It was a visual tug-of-war and for the moment, it was a draw, but one grounded in respect. "Sometimes crutches are all we have until we can stand up on our own again."

Impatience clawed at him. Brent blew out a breath, trying to maintain control over his emotions, which threatened to burst out and go all over the board. "I know you mean well—"

She placed a gentling hand on his arm. He looked down at it, then at her. Callie kept it where it was. "I mean more than that, Brent. I mean to find her." Withdrawing her hand, she let it drop to her side. "Now, shall we get started?"

Brent squared his shoulders, telling himself to focus on the task ahead and not what it might ultimately mean. That one of the people within the case files had his precious girl. "Right."

They'd been at it for hours, sorting through files, with Brent first making a judgment call and then Callie considering it. The list of people to investigate began to form.

The filing cabinet drawers had turned out to be crammed full of cases. She'd discovered to her amusement that Brent preferred to deal with paper rather than computers, opting to make his notes in pen rather than type them on a keyboard, to be printed out. In a high-tech world, he was still, at bottom, an old-fashioned guy.

The stack of viable contenders who might want to exact revenge on him had grown steadily over the past four hours.

Leaning back in her chair and rubbing the bridge of her nose, Callie willed away the headache that threatened to overtake her. For the moment it appeared to listen. Or maybe it was just lying in wait for an opportune moment to strike, announcing its presence with a chorus of drums throbbing at her temples. She'd take what respite she could get.

She glanced at the file opened on her lap. Brent's handwriting was a challenge at times. "You know, this might have been a lot easier if all this was on your hard drive." She indicated the dormant computer on his desk, which she was beginning to suspect was nothing more than a glorified, overly large paperweight on steroids.

He looked in the direction of the machine with something less than respectful regard. Carmella had spent hours trying to get him to at least learn the basics. It wasn't that he couldn't; he wouldn't. There had to be a place for the human touch in this high-tech world of theirs. In his opinion, people relied too much on computers. If there was ever a power shortage, the entire world outside the Australian outback would grind to a sudden, jarring halt.

He shrugged. "My eyes get tired, looking at the screen. I've never been much of an electronics junkie," he confessed in a moment of honesty. He knew most men thrived on the things that left him cold. Brent reached for the cup of coffee that had long since passed the point of lukewarm. "An embarrassment to my gender, I suppose. But the sight of a fifty-inch screen never turned me on."

Her energy level was ebbing away quickly. Since he had opened up this avenue of conversation, she decided to draw him out a little. Remind him that he was not just a judge and a justifiably concerned parent, but a human being with likes and dislikes, as well.

Still leaning back in the chair, she studied him. He

had the face of a leader and the soul to match. But even leaders had outside interests. "Just for the record, what does turn you on?"

The answer came as if it were part of a word-association quiz. "Tulips."

The last thing she expected to do sitting here, looking through five years' worth of files for a possible kidnapper, was grin. The headache circling her head hovered somewhere between oblivion and attack as she looked at Brent.

"Excuse me? Did you just say 'tulips'?"

He'd never seen her grin before. It made her seem younger than her years, as if she was just playing dress-up in her mother's clothes and was really still just a young girl instead of a police detective. Was he placing his faith in the wrong person? God, he hoped not.

"You find that amusing?"

She lifted a shoulder, letting it drop carelessly. "That depends on whether you like growing them or getting them."

A smattering of a smile, far smaller than anything gracing her lips, emerged on his. He hadn't thought he was capable of smiling after this morning.

"Growing them. It relaxes me." Jennifer had thought he was crazy, telling him gardening was a hobby for boring housewives and old men. But Rachel had liked sitting beside him, digging in the earth with the small shovel he'd gotten her. "There's something very basic about getting back to nature, about getting your hands dirty and nurturing seed-

lings along until they germinate into something beautiful.'' He looked at her, half expecting a sarcastic
comment. ''Does that surprise you?''

She debated a polite answer, but knew that he
would respect honesty more. So she was honest.
''Frankly, yes. I wouldn't have thought of you as the
kind of man who liked 'getting his hands dirty.' I
pictured you with a squadron of gardeners to get
dirty for you.''

He didn't have far to look to know the origin of
that image. He was well acquainted with it. Had been
schooled in it when he was young.

''Ah, yes, the good old Montgomery legacy.'' It
was said that none of his recent ancestors actually
knew the meaning of an honest day's toil. They'd all
been lawyers to the rich and celebrated. He doubted
if any of them even knew the first name of any of
the people who worked for them. ''We're not all
cookie-cutter identical.''

She could hear the annoyance in his voice. At least
she'd momentarily redirected his attention from the
kidnapping, although she hadn't meant to get his annoyance focused on her. ''Sorry, I didn't mean to
offend you.''

''No, I'm the one who's sorry. I'm usually better
at keeping my temper in check.'' Unable to remain
seated any longer, he got up, shoving his fisted hands
deep into his pockets. Hitting nothing. Wanting to hit
something. Wanting more than anything to hit this
man who had destroyed his world. ''It's just that I
feel so damn helpless, so damn impotent.'' He stared

out the window. It had long since gotten dark outside. Evening shadows sat where cars had been parked earlier. Brent's voice was small, tight, as he added, "There's nothing I can do."

Rising, she came up behind him. Feeling for him. "You're doing it," she contradicted. "You're going through cases, looking for a possible suspect."

It was beginning to feel like an exercise in futility. He turned to look at the piles on his desk. "About twenty percent of these cases represent possible suspects." His words were dressed in frustration. He gestured toward the filing cabinets they had emptied. "I really doubt there are many people in there who wish me well."

But that was exactly why they were going through the files in the first place. "Wishing and doing are two very different things."

He turned completely around to face her. Surprised at how near she was. "So, in your opinion, wishing isn't the very first step toward doing."

"A lot of times, no." She laughed softly, a tired, resigned laugh that had somehow not gotten lost amid the exasperation she had faced today. "Otherwise, there'd be a lot more dead people out there for the police to process." The scent of his cologne seemed to descend on her out of nowhere. Callie remembered the electric charge she'd felt when she'd danced with him that night. It was so vivid, she could swear she felt the remnants now. "There'd also be a great many more infidelities."

Callie raised her eyes to his as she said the latter,

not completely sure of just what she was doing. Or why.

Maybe it was the hour and the fact that when she was tired, her defenses, always so rigidly in place, tended to slip just a little. Enough to make her think of herself as vulnerable.

It was the last thing in the world she wanted to be. And he was the last man on earth she had a right to be feeling this way with. The man was fighting desperation, trying to find his daughter before it was too late. He needed a crack detective at the top of her game helping him, not a woman who was feeling odd stirrings in his company.

Yet there it was. She was feeling something.

She was feeling.

The realization slammed itself against her like a loose newspaper page suddenly being blown against a windshield.

It took her breath away.

She hadn't felt anything for a very, very long time.

He laughed shortly. "Not everyone subscribes to your theory."

Very few times did she speak before her brain was engaged, but this was one of those times. "You mean your ex-wife?"

When Brent looked at her, his eyes somber, she realized that she'd crossed some line she shouldn't have, but there was no way to retreat gracefully to the other side.

She shrugged in what she hoped was a casual manner. "There were rumors."

Yes, he damn well figured there would have been. Not because he was a judge, but because he was a Montgomery. "What kind of rumors?"

She blunted the edge. And gave it her own spin. Not just to be kind, but because it was what she believed. It was one of those nonsecret secrets that Brent Montgomery's wife had been unfaithful to him. "That your ex-wife didn't know what she had. That she didn't belong in your circle."

One minute the woman before him was coming across tough as nails, the next minute she was soft. Brent couldn't exactly read her. But he knew what she was doing now.

"You're making that up to spare my feelings. I know what they said. That I couldn't keep Jennifer satisfied. That she found me boring." The latter had been an accusation she'd hurled at him when he'd confronted her with the name of her lover.

Jennifer Montgomery needed her head examined and her eyes checked. And an MRI to find her missing heart wouldn't have been out of the question, either, Callie thought.

Knowing that this had to make him feel uncomfortable, she took it out of the realm of personal. "I read somewhere that Taylor Madison's first wife said the same thing about him." She shrugged, mentioning the latest Hollywood heartthrob to grace the fantasies of women everywhere. "Go figure. Me, I think that he's one of the nicest men in the world."

Brent raised an eyebrow, mildly surprised. "You know him?"

Callie shook her head "Just what I read." She didn't want to sound like some mindless fan. It was her instincts that came into play here, just as they did with him. "Sometimes you don't have to know a person inside and out to have an educated opinion."

Suddenly she realized they were standing so close there wasn't enough room for a whisper between them now. Another moment, and—

What the hell was she doing, her brain thundered, finally ushering in the hovering headache full force. This was the parent of a kidnapping victim, not her latest date she was talking to.

Maybe that was the problem. She didn't have a latest date. Hadn't had any date at all, not since Kyle was killed. Her family had been urging her for the past six months to set her grief aside and begin going out again, but she just couldn't get herself to do it. Couldn't gather up the will, the courage, to get back on a horse that could possibly throw her again. Or maybe even get stuck at the starting gate.

And yet…

And yet she was a normal woman with hormones that reacted to a good-looking man. Like the man standing right before her. But one didn't live by hormones alone, she argued fiercely.

Her temples throbbing, her pulse inexplicably scrambling, Callie pulled back, stumbling inwardly as she retreated. Her eyes never left his face even though she wanted to look away. "It's getting late. Neither one of us is thinking clearly."

Was she talking about his daughter's case, or what had almost happened here? Because if she hadn't had the sense to pull back, Brent knew he would have kissed her. Kissed her because he needed the comfort of a human touch, of compassion turned his way.

Of he didn't know what.

He'd always been the strong one, no matter the situation. The one who, though not overtly an optimist, had always held things together by sheer grit. Because he had to. It was a matter of honor. He hadn't allowed himself to get swept away by his family's name or his family's wealth, the way his cousin Hamilton had. At thirty-eight, Hamilton had yet to grow up, yet to become a responsible adult. Brent had always been determined to make something of himself even if he didn't have to. Not for the family name, certainly not for his distant parents, who only required from him a lack of scandal, but for himself.

And, for a time, for Jennifer.

But now the focus of his world was Rachel. And she had been stolen from him.

"No," he agreed slowly, "we're not."

He dragged a hand through his hair as he put space between them. Space because that vulnerability, that weakness that had made him want to kiss her was still there. Begging for companionship, for fulfillment. For all the earthly emotional comforts that seeking solace from someone in the most intimate fashion created.

Feeling uncharacteristically unsteady, Callie finally looked away.

"Do you mind if I take these?" She nodded at the stack of possible suspects they had compiled. "I want to go through them more thoroughly, see if anything further leaps out at me."

"Then you're not going to investigate them?"

She hadn't meant to give him the wrong impression. "Oh, yes, every one of them. Even the ones in prison." Just because a person was in prison didn't mean he or she couldn't reach out and arrange for a heinous crime to be committed in their name. It wasn't just the arm of the law that was long, but the criminals, as well. She looked down at the files. "I just wanted some alone time with them. I'll bring them back tomorrow." As she spoke, she began making out a list of the files she was taking with her. Callie glanced up at him, a half smile on her lips. "I promise."

"No need to promise, I find you eminently trustworthy, Detective Cavanaugh." The formal edge from his voice faded as he added, "And I'm glad you're the one working on this case."

That caught her off guard. "Why?"

"You're not the only one who hears rumors." He pulled the drapes closed. "You have a reputation of never giving up." Brent crossed back to her. "Right now I need someone like that on my team."

"Rachel's team," she corrected. And because it was about a child, it galvanized all of them on a task force that much more firmly. "This is all about your little girl, and none of us are going to rest until we find her." She could see what he was thinking.

"Alive," she added to chase away the look on his face.

A small, grateful smile curved his lips as he nodded his head. "Thank you. You know, I didn't realize how weak I was until this morning."

"Weak?" That was the last word she would have applied to him.

But it was the way he thought of himself right now. He was vainly trying to suppress an all-pervasive, weak-in-the-knees feeling. "Part of me feels like everything inside is collapsing."

Figuratively, she'd held more than her share of hands. "The other part is filled with rage, right?"

She'd picked the right word, Brent thought. *Rage.* Pure, white-hot rage. It undulated through him now. "How did you—?"

"You're not my first distraught parent," Callie replied. "And the rage helps balance things out inside, putting everything on a more even keel. But you're not weak." The list finished, she handed it to him and picked up the files, tucking them against her chest. "You're just human. I can tell you that if you didn't feel this way, then you'd be right up there on the top of our suspect list."

"So you've cleared me?" It was a rhetorical question. He assumed she had. Crossing to the doorway, he held the door open for her. When she stepped through, he locked it behind her.

The floor looked deserted. Only every other light was on, part of the energy conservation push that was going on in California.

"No, you cleared you," she corrected as they walked toward the elevator. "I just listened to the facts as you talked."

That was a relief, he supposed. He couldn't imagine a worse situation than having the police think that he was involved in any other way than he actually was. He pressed for the elevator, then looked at the files she was holding. Was she also inadvertently holding Rachel's fate in her hands, as well?

"Do you really think he's in there?"

That was the sixty-four-million-dollar question. "If he is, we'll find him."

"That's not what I asked."

She wasn't going to insult Brent by giving him a definite answer without a solid foundation. She liked to pick her occasions for that, and she had already sworn to him that he'd be reunited with his daughter, something logically she knew she couldn't really promise.

So instead, she gave him the rationale behind the search. "I think it's highly likely. And right now, it's our best bet."

He nodded, knowing he couldn't ask for more. Other than getting Rachel back.

The black-and-white container of Rocky Road ice cream was leaving an irregular sweat ring on her coffee table. For the moment, engrossed in what she was reading, Callie had forgotten that it was even there. Ice cream, diet soda and M&Ms were her diet of choice every time she became entrenched in a case.

She knew that it would have driven her father wild if he knew, but then, the preponderance of her meals were taken at the house and he saw to it that she was well fed most of the time.

Desperate times called for desperate food.

Her feet curled under her, Callie sat on her sofa, the files divided into two piles on the coffee table, safely out of the range of the ice cream container with its spreading sweat ring. One pile contained the more dominant suspects, the ones Brent thought of as more dangerous.

The people within the files comprised a spectrum of humanity. Not all were hardened criminals. She'd noted that there was even a disgraced former computer CEO in the lot. He'd actually been the judge's first case. Not a very pleasant man to deal with according to the file. One of those creatures who believed himself superior to the general population. He was also one of the ones who was currently in prison. She couldn't see the man engineering a jailbreak to get back at the man who'd sent him away. He was more the type to earn himself a law degree and argue his way out just to show up Brent.

Still, she'd go see him, or send one of the others on the task force to do it. As she would all the other people in the files on her coffee table. Every possible lead had to be looked into. Just like every call that came in from well-meaning citizens had to be heard to, logged and checked out.

Putting the file down on the sofa next to her, she reached for the container. The spoon she'd left in it, its lower edge buried in a rock-solid portion of chocolate, was now listing to one side, its foundation softening to the consistency of hard pudding. She didn't care. She was partial to ice cream soup, sometimes preferred it. Took the effort out of chipping away at a frozen portion of ice cream for the next mouthful.

Dark-blue eyes suddenly flashed through her mind. Sad dark-blue eyes.

She had no business sitting here feeding her face, when he was home, worried out of his mind, and his little girl was who knew where.

With a sigh Callie got up to return the container to the freezer before she had a pool of Rocky Road on her coffee table, then made a beeline for the files.

On her way to the kitchen, she noticed that it was after one in the morning. No rest for the weary, she thought. She wondered if Brent had managed to fall asleep yet, and if he had, if he could sleep peacefully.

With the softened container of ice cream now butted up against a stack of frozen vegetables, Callie returned to the sofa and the remaining files she had yet to study.

The long night got longer.

Chapter 6

Callie woke up to the sound of Brent's voice. Or rather, to the ringing of the telephone, which, once she finished fumbling for the receiver buried under a file on her nightstand, led her to the sound of the judge's baritone voice.

"Any news?"

Realizing that her eyes were still shut, Callie pried them open and tried to focus. On the room and on the question.

Bits and pieces of last night returned, falling into place like a kaleidoscope rolling down a hill. The image kept changing, but the kaleidoscope remained a given. Callie glanced down. She'd fallen asleep in her clothes again, propped up against a mountain of pillows on her bed, surrounded by the files. Hoping there was such a thing as osmosis when it came to

breakthroughs because, heaven knew, she wasn't
making any the regular way.

Taking care not to send any of the files tumbling
to the floor, Callie sat up slowly and dragged a hand
through her hair, pushing it away from her face.
There was a syrupy taste in her mouth that had turned
sickeningly sweet. One last hit of Rocky Road before
trudging off to the bedroom was the culprit responsible. She ran her tongue along her teeth, willing the
taste away. When would she learn?

"No," she told Brent, hating the fact that she had
nothing new to tell him, no new lifeline, however
thin, to toss him. "I'm sorry."

Callie heard him attempt to suppress a sigh. He
was less than successful. The sound of his breath
rippled through her. As did the short, scratchy noise
that followed. His stubble rubbing against the mouthpiece, she guessed. It had an intimate sound that
pulled a response from her she didn't want touched.

Get hold of yourself, Cavanaugh, she silently ordered, exasperated.

Of all the times to have her barriers need retooling,
she couldn't have picked a worse one. Whatever at-
traction she might have once had for Brent Montgomery was going to have to be pushed into the
background again until all this was over. Anything
else wasn't ethical.

Blinking, she looked at the wristwatch she never
removed except for the length of time it took her to
take a shower. "I'll be heading into the office in
about ninety minutes, let me call you from there.

Better yet, meet me,'' she suggested. ''I've got a few questions to ask you about this motley crew.''

''Motley crew?''

Tucking the receiver against her ear, she began gathering up the files before they had a chance to spill their contents on the bed and mingle. ''The people in the case files.''

''I'll be there.''

It would give him a direction to go in, Brent thought, hanging up. Something to focus on. God knew he needed that.

His sister and brother-in-law had tried to persuade him to come stay with them at their house. He'd politely but firmly turned them down. He knew they were both concerned, both meant well, but he didn't want to be subjected to their barely veiled looks of sympathy and compassion. He couldn't deal with that. He wanted nothing more right now than to just operate on automatic pilot, moving ever forward until he could sweep his daughter back into his arms.

Automatic pilot meant getting less than three hours of sleep.

He'd sleep once Rachel was back.

Brent looked down at the receiver he'd just replaced on his desk. He supposed he should try reaching Jennifer again, although the first two attempts had been futile. Brent sighed. He didn't need any added frustration, however minor.

Contact with Jennifer was never minor frustration, he reminded himself. No matter how cool and even-tempered he tried to be, with Jennifer it always felt as if there was a major blowup on the way. Jennifer knew how to push every single wrong button in his makeup. It was obviously a gift.

But, like it or not, she was Rachel's mother, and she deserved to hear the news from him before he held the press conference he'd been putting off. It was scheduled for nine this morning in front of the police station.

Maybe it had been the wrong thing to do, not going to the press immediately, but he'd held on to the hope that Rachel could be found without his resorting to a public appeal. It was against his nature to willingly draw the huge volume of media attention that one of these cases always attracted. Attention and nut cases. He'd tried so hard to shield Rachel, to create a perfect world for her.

Or as perfect as was possible with only one parent emotionally available to her.

With a sigh, he reached for the telephone and tapped out first Jennifer's home number and then the one that connected him to her cell phone. The first got him the same answering machine recording he'd already listened to twice before. There was no point in leaving another message. She obviously hadn't received, or at the very least, chosen not to answer either of them.

The second number only put him in touch with the same annoying message he'd received each time he called. That she was either not answering or out of the service provider's area.

The latter was probably the case. Jennifer was supposed to be off somewhere in Nevada on vacation. Nothing ever got in the way of her having a good time, he thought with uncustomary bitterness. He had no idea exactly where his ex-wife was. That information hadn't been forthcoming from her, not that he'd wanted it at the time. He wouldn't even have known she was going to Nevada if she hadn't let it slip to Rachel during the last minute of a parental visit she'd paid the girl over a month ago.

He listened to the cell message, frowning. He had more important things to do than stand here, listening to disembodied recordings prevent him from making any human contact.

Slamming down the receiver in its cradle, Brent went to get dressed.

When he didn't spend too much time bugging her about the fact that she looked tired, something she knew for a fact to be evident at first glance despite her artful application of makeup, or that she'd arrived late for breakfast again, Callie knew something was up with her father. It wasn't like him not to make continual suggestions and observations.

She knew she should count her blessings and get going right after she'd paid her obligatory visit and consumed a piece of toast, but Callie couldn't just leave him this way.

So she lingered over her breakfast, waiting until Rayne and the twins filed out. Patrick and Patience, who'd put in a quick appearance earlier that morning, had already left. Shaw had never shown up. The case he was working on had taken him down to L.A. and he'd wanted to get a quick jump on traffic.

As if that was possible in California.

Callie watched while her youngest sister kissed Andrew goodbye and then closed the door behind her. She turned and gave her father a long, penetrating look, the same one he gave her whenever he was digging. "Okay, Dad, tell me what gives."

Andrew avoided her eyes as he dumped the large frying pan into the sink. Hot water met the greasy surface. "What do you mean?"

"You didn't bother giving me the third-degree this morning. About anything."

He looked at her over his shoulder as he placed the pan on the counter, to be washed later. "Would it have helped?"

She talked only when she wanted to. She was as stubborn as he was that way. "No."

"Maybe it's an old dog learning new tricks."

Ha, that would be the day. Callie held up one finger, "One, you're not an old dog and two," a second finger joined the first, "you already know every trick in the book."

The disgruntled expression didn't leave his face. "I guess those are supposed to be compliments."

"Observations." Because she was feeling too much energy to just stand still, even in her tired state, Callie began to clear the table. "Now, I want to know. What's wrong?"

He stopped moving around to look at the calendar before looking at her. "You know what today is?"

She blew out a breath as she thought for a second. "Wednesday? Two weeks away from Halloween?" But even as she said the last sentence, it dawned on her, going off in her head like a delayed flash from a still camera. "It's Mom's birthday."

Andrew nodded, trying not to notice that even after all these years his throat still filled up at the thought of being without Rose. "She would have been fifty today." Facing the window, he looked out sadly across the backyard, a backyard that had once been privy to such happy times. "And I would have teased her mercilessly about it."

Callie gently laid a hand on her father's shoulder. Even at his age the man still had a powerful build. He'd always been such a source of strength for her. She wished she could give him some of hers right now. It touched her with both pride and anguish that he still missed her mother after all this time. Another man would have long ago found someone else to fill the space. Still, it hurt to see him alone. One day all of them were going to be gone and the house would be empty. He needed someone his own age to be with.

"Dad, you can't keep doing this to yourself."

Andrew cleared his throat. He didn't usually wallow in self-pity. That wasn't like him. Drawing himself up, he turned his attention to his firstborn daughter. It was about his kids, it was always about his kids. They were what had kept him going all these years.

That, and the hope that Rose was alive somewhere.

He snorted at her advice. "Said the one who's still grieving after a whole year's gone by." He pinned her with a look. "You've got your whole life ahead of you, kiddo. Don't waste it."

Callie withdrew her hand and stepped back, shaking her head. She might have known. "How did this get to be a conversation about me?"

Andrew winked at her. "Didn't you know? Every conversation is about you."

"I've got to get going." Bracing her hand on his shoulder, she reached up and brushed a kiss against his cheek. "Maybe I'll stop by tonight and we'll do something."

"Maybe," he agreed, knowing that even though she meant it, she wouldn't be by. When Callie was on a case, she became consumed with it.

Just the way he'd always been.

Walking her to the back door, Andrew watched her leave, then closed the door behind her. He glanced at the dishes in the sink and along the counter, waiting to be prepared for the dishwasher. Leaving them where they were, he went to his den. Where the missing person's file was spread out across his desk.

The one with his wife's name on it.

Hurrying through the parking lot, Callie recognized Brent's car parked in the section marked Visitors just before she reached the building. Brent was here already. Her heart surprised her by doing something akin to a hiccup in her chest.

Maybe she was going through a second adolescence, she thought disparagingly. She'd told him to meet her here, hadn't she? What was the matter with her?

If this was what lack of sleep did, she was going to have to make a point of getting at least four hours a night, otherwise, she wasn't going to be of any decent use to anyone.

Muttering under her breath, she headed up the stone steps and into the five-story building.

Callie made a point of stopping by the forensic lab before she went to her office. Any information they'd come up with from the crime scene would be more than she had at her disposal at the moment.

The head pathologist shook his head in response to her question. "Not much yet, we're still processing our findings from the autopsy. There's a partial imprint of a grill on the woman's chest." Callie tried not to shiver as she listened. "Looks like the kidnapper might have been driving a Mercedes."

She noted that the man was safely surrounding himself with words that couldn't be pinned down yet. "A kidnapper in a Mercedes, now there's something you don't hear about every day. Any idea what model?"

"We're working on it."

"Can't ask for more than that," she murmured. "Let me know the minute you have anything."

"Goes without saying." The man had already gone back to his work.

Pleased finally to have something, however small,

to offer, Callie lengthened her stride, heading to her own floor. Too impatient to wait for the elevator, which always seemed to be somewhere else and took its time reaching her, she used the stairs.

A sudden need for coffee had her redirecting her steps toward the vending machine. Everything always went better with coffee.

It wasn't the vending machine's finest hour. It served the coffee before the paper cup. Callie knew that a second monetary offering would only bring about the same results. She had no alternative open to her but to face Will Durango's coffee.

Divorced, with no children and relatively no life to speak of, the burglary and homicide detective was always the first one in the office every morning, and for some unknown reason he liked his coffee to taste like three-day-old ashes garnered from a smelting oven.

Still, heated ashes was better than no coffee at all. Resigned, she stopped to pour some of the barely flowing tar into her mug and plunked her coins in the metal can beside the coffee machine.

All things considered, she mused, it was Durango who should have been paying them for tolerating what he did with coffee. Asking him to lighten up or use a sparing hand never got anyone anywhere.

Fortified, she turned around. Only lightning reflexes had her pulling back before she bumped into Seth Adams and sent the contents of her mug making contact with his chest.

The five-foot-nine detective took a step back, recovering. Until last month he'd been her partner, but unlike the scenarios that were so popular in the movies and on TV, they didn't get along. It didn't take long for Callie to see that there was something about her being a woman that rubbed him the wrong way. She knew that having her in charge of this investigation was quickly rubbing his skin raw.

She didn't like the look in his eyes. The tentative apology over the near collision faded from her lips.

"See you've got a new partner."

Callie almost asked what he was talking about, then realized that Brent was probably waiting for her by her desk. There was no doubt in her mind that Adams already knew that she and the judge had spent a good part of the evening in his chambers. Her ex-partner always liked being on top of things. That had been one of the major sore points from early on. Because one of the things he wanted to be on top of was her.

She looked at him coolly. "The captain said it was okay to keep the judge in the loop. Judge Montgomery's father and the captain go way back."

Steely blue eyes stared at her intently. "Maybe that's the problem. Maybe that's what's impeding this investigation."

Since the investigation was less than twenty-four hours old and progressing as fast as it could, all things considered, Callie hadn't a clue what the snide remark was referring to. But knowing Adams, it couldn't be good. "What do you mean?"

"Okay." His tone was patronizing. She tried hard

not to bristle. "Let me paint you another scenario." The moment he began talking, she realized Adams must have seen her preliminary report, clearing Brent. The detective's approach to life was simple: everyone was tainted. She was certain that he had skeletons of his own, but for now, no one knew just where they were buried. "Our grieving father back there does some very unfatherly things with his little girl. He comes to his senses, or more likely, thinks he's been discovered. This could ruin his career, his life, so he takes steps to fix the situation. The nanny might be the only one who can point a finger at him, so he does away with her, takes the kid to make it look like a kidnapping and disposes of her to make sure she keeps her mouth shut. Public sympathy, no scandal. Best of all worlds. End of story." He gave her a look. "He wouldn't be the first father to get too close to his offspring."

For a split second she felt like punching him, but that would only have made her look like an emotional female and play right into his hands. She thanked God she'd managed to convince the captain to reassign Adams to someone else. As a rule, the captain didn't like to be told how to run his department.

With effort she reminded herself that at times Adams had his moments and was more than a decent investigator. But this wasn't one of those moments. And "decent" had nothing to do with the situation.

"No, not this man." She stood her ground. "I'm not buying it."

"Why? Because he's a judge?" He cocked his head, a smirk on his lips. "Or because you know him?"

She knew he wasn't talking about acquaintances. To Adams the only way people knew each other was in the carnal sense. "The first part has nothing to do with it. Men in high places fall all the time."

"Then it's because you know him."

She wasn't about to have him relish even a moment of triumph here. The next thing she knew, he would be spreading rumors about her and Brent. As if the man didn't have enough to contend with.

"I know my gut," she contradicted. "And it tells me that this man is on the level. He loves that little girl more than life itself. I can see it in his eyes," she added when Adams was about to discount her intuition.

The look in Adams's eyes bordered on a leer as he regarded her. "What else do you see in his eyes?"

She was dying to tell the man where to go, but again that would be giving in to a fit of temper. She divorced herself from any emotion as she said, "Pain, a hell of a lot of pain. Now if you're through spinning alternative theories, Adams, maybe you might give a thought to getting back to doing something that might help us find that little girl."

One hand wrapped around his own mug of coffee, Adams raised the other in mock surrender. "Hey, you're the primary on this one."

And it was eating him up, she thought, knowing that taking orders from a woman stuck in Adams's throat. "Yes, I am. Now why don't you put in some time fielding phone calls? I'm sure after the judge's press conference the phones'll be ringing off the hook."

"And what will you and the judge be doing until the press conference?" he asked. Sarcasm fairly dripped from his voice. "I saw His Honor hovering around your desk."

"We're going over the list of people he sentenced who might have it in for him." To underscore her point, she nodded at the files she was still holding.

"The captain's in this morning. That means you're going to have to find yourself a new cozy place to hole up in."

Enough was enough. Even at her best, Callie wasn't in the mood to put up with Adams, and she was far from her best right now. "Look, Adams, you have something to say, get it out in the open now. Otherwise, get back to work."

Again, he held up his hand in surrender and began backing away.

"Yes, ma'am." Giving her a smart salute, the detective turned away from her and went back into the squad room.

Ass, she thought tartly. It was all she could do to keep from shouting the word after him. But instead she took a deep cleansing breath, let it out again and centered herself. It was time to get back to the only thing that mattered.

Finding Rachel Montgomery.

* * *

Brent knew it was probably ridiculous, but he could feel his heart tighten in his chest the moment he saw Callie walking into the room that had been turned into the gathering point for his daughter's task force. There was no earthly reason to hope that something had happened between the time he'd talked to her earlier and now, something good that would lead him to his daughter. And hoping certainly wasn't his style.

But he hoped nonetheless.

Hoped that this long-legged, take-charge blonde in the dark-green jacket and skirt would take away the pain he'd been living with since yesterday morning, or at least ease it. After all, she'd been the one who'd created it in the first place by telling him his daughter had been kidnapped. Hers had been the voice that had set his world completely off-kilter.

Every nerve ending he possessed went on alert. She had something, he could tell.

It was there in her eyes, a nugget of hope. It began to stoke the ashes in his chest, coaxing out a flicker of a flame, however weak. He wanted to run to her, but forced himself to stand still. The longer he waited, the longer he could pretend it was going to be all right.

Callie started talking the second she got within Brent's hearing range, ignoring the fact that Adams was standing on the sidelines, supposedly looking at the back bulletin board. The large one that accommodated some of their major data and the time line that had yet to be filled in. Right now what dominated the board was the photograph of Rachel that had been distributed to every single set of eyes within a five-mile radius.

And what dominated Callie's attention was the expression on Brent's face. He looked hopeful. She wished she had more to tell him.

Chapter 7

"The medical examiner found a partial grill impression on Miss Culhane's body," Callie said as she approached him. "The CSI team thinks it belongs to a Mercedes. They're trying to narrow that down for us."

"A Mercedes?" Brent echoed incredulously. "He must have stolen it."

"Probably." Callie stopped at her desk. There were twenty of them on the task force so far, with more promised manpower on the way. Right now the room looked like the center of LAX. People were coming and going, and the din steadily grew. "We'll look into any reports of a Mercedes being stolen around the time of the kidnapping."

He still couldn't come to terms with the word. He dealt with crime every day, was surrounded by criminals accused of all sorts of heinous acts. Through it all, he'd managed to maintain an inner sanctum, a haven for himself and his daughter. And now that was gone.

"But what good will that do?" he wanted to know. "That still doesn't get us to the kidnapper. Anyone could have stolen the Mercedes."

She knew how frustrating it had to be for him. Which was why she had always tried to keep herself divorced from what was happening. Emotions only caused a person to make mistakes. But in this case, it was hard not to get involved.

Callie glanced over and saw that Adams had given up the pretense of looking at a file and was watching them. She turned her back on the man. "We keep gathering facts and trying to piece them together. It's a little like one of those thousand-piece puzzles. When you start out, there're only all these pieces that don't look as if they'll ever come together. But in the end, you've got a whole picture."

"The difference there," Brent pointed out, "is that you start out knowing what the puzzle is supposed to look like. We still have no idea who took Rachel and killed Delia."

"But we will," she assured him with as much conviction as she could infuse into her tone. "The challenge might be greater, but my team's up to it." She shifted, holding out the files she'd taken home with her. "I went over these files again last night, and I have a few questions that might help us narrow down the scope somewhat. Are you game?"

He wanted to leap, to fly, but all that could be done was to take tiny baby steps. From where he stood, it felt impossible to reach journey's end. Resigned, he nodded. ''Lead the way.''

Callie looked over to the glass-enclosed office at the far end of the room. Captain D'Angelo, a tall, thin man with silver-gray hair and an aptitude for keeping peace among the ranks, was standing there, talking to one of the detectives. She couldn't use his office again.

''The captain's in today. We're going to have to use one of the interrogation rooms.'' There were six on the floor. Windowless rooms meant to make you feel as if you were sealed off from the immediate world. She wasn't sure how Brent would react to being in one. ''You okay with that?''

''I'm okay with anything that gets us closer to finding Rachel.'' Because time was precious, he glanced at his watch.

Callie began to lead the way out of the task force room. She looked at him over her shoulder. ''Don't worry, I'll have you downstairs in time for the press conference.''

He'd only talked to Captain D'Angelo about appealing to the public for help earlier this morning. The captain had promised he would handle everything. ''You know about that?''

She flashed a smile at him that did more than just hearten Brent. But there was no time for him to dwell on anything else. Not now. Not when his daughter needed him.

"I keep up," she told him.

She did more than that. She stayed ahead. Which was what allowed him to continue holding on to the slender thread of hope.

Forty-five minutes later, Callie's questions answered, Brent walked out of the interrogation room behind her. He'd found the room somewhat claustrophobic. He could see how, after a while, a suspect might feel as if the very walls were closing in on him.

Or maybe it was the situation that made him feel that way.

He watched Callie as she called several members of the task force over and divided the possible suspects among them. Out of all the files, twelve men and three women had emerged as viable contenders. Each was going to have to be tracked down and checked out.

No stone unturned, he thought. But there were so many stones and so little time.

He tried not to think about it, about what life would be like without Rachel if they couldn't find her. He wasn't going to allow that to become an option, even if he had to move heaven and earth himself in order to finally find her.

The last of the files distributed, Callie turned back toward him.

"We'd better get you down for that press conference." She walked quickly with him to the elevator. The doors opened as if the car had been waiting there all along. "Just for the record," leaning over, Callie pressed for the first floor, "none of the suspects drives a Mercedes. Eight don't have access to any sort of moving vehicle at all, unless it might be the prison laundry wagon."

"But you're having them checked out?"

"Every possibility is being examined," she assured him.

The elevator car stopped, but he made no move to get out. Instead he looked at her. "Tell me we're going to find her."

The vulnerability in his eyes took her aback. He was such a powerful-looking man, the contrast was astounding. She was surprised that he allowed her to see it. "We're going to find her."

He nodded. The moment evaporating, he squared his shoulders and walked to the lobby where the news media had converged with their microphones and their cameras, eager to help, eager to be part of this latest tragedy.

Callie hung back. This was the captain's area. In general, she thought of the Fourth Estate as being comprised predominantly of vultures who fed on the sorrows and misfortunes of the average man and woman. Their enthusiasm for being the first with breaking news often caused them to lose sight of the fact that there were people with hearts behind each story.

But if the reporters could help by making the general public aware of the particulars, if having Rachel Montgomery's photograph plastered across every screen in California could help in finding the little girl, then venturing out amid the vultures was a small enough price to pay.

She would have done it herself if it hadn't been for the captain. Luckily, Captain D'Angelo took to the sight of a video camera like a duck to water.

As she stood on the sidelines, Callie listened to the judge make an impassioned plea to the kidnapper to take out any grievance the man or woman had on him and not on his innocent daughter.

Brent was a private man, a man accustomed to keeping his own counsel. She knew this had to be hard on him. Harder still was making an appeal to the public for help, to come forward with any information, however small, that they had. He asked them to consider the matter carefully because perhaps they didn't know that they knew some important detail. He closed by going over the approximate time and the exact location of the accident.

The moment he ended his appeal, questions came flying at him like bees swarming around the entrance of a hive. Bearing up to it, Brent fielded them all. Until one reporter threw him a question about Jennifer.

"Do you think your ex-wife might be behind the kidnapping?"

That door opened, the other reporters didn't give him a chance to answer. Instead, more questions came, fast and furious.

"Where is she, Judge? Why isn't she here?"

"This is an election year, Judge. All this attention, do you think it can help your reelection?"

Callie had begun to move forward as soon as Jennifer's name had been mentioned. She saw Brent's eyes grow progressively colder with each question. The press conference was turning in directions they hadn't foreseen. From a genuine life-and-death situation to something that had the makings of a tabloid melodrama.

The captain stepped in to divert the media's attention. Callie saw her moment and came up to Brent. Taking hold of his arm, she drew him quickly away from the podium.

"Let's get out of here," she urged. "You've done all the good you can."

Without waiting for his reply, still holding on to his arm, she forged a path back to the elevators. Several reporters broke off from the crowd and followed in their wake.

The elevator car was standing open. Getting in, Callie quickly pressed for the doors to close. Once they did, she sighed with relief and pressed the button to get them back to her floor.

"Thanks." His deep voice boomed behind her.

Callie smiled in his direction. "Thought you might need a breather before we wound up having to peel your fingers off the throat of that obnoxious reporter." She referred to the one who'd asked about the upcoming reelection.

"The thought crossed my mind," he admitted.

The doors opened on Callie's floor and they got out. "When are they releasing Delia's body?"

The CSI team had gotten every shred of evidence they could from the hit-and-run victim's body. All that remained was to have the release papers signed. "Probably a little later today, why?"

"She has no family. I thought I'd arrange for a funeral service for her."

Callie stopped short of her desk to look at him. "If she has no family, and no friends from what we could see, who's the service for?"

The answer was simple. "Delia."

Callie nodded, understanding. She was more than a little impressed. With his own world in utter, devastating turmoil, Brent could still manage to think of a woman who so many would have easily and completely put out of their minds.

"I'll talk to the M.E. and see if I can speed things up," she promised.

He smiled to himself as the live broadcast ended and an announcement was made that the station was returning to its originally scheduled programming. The press conference had interrupted all the shows in their usual time slots. Even the local cable stations carried the broadcast.

Switching from channel to channel, he could see the anguish in the judge's eyes from all different angles.

Good. He was suffering. Just as the self-righteous bastard had made him suffer.

"Won't do you any good, Montgomery," he said to the image that was no longer there. "Nobody saw anything. Nobody's going to help you."

Turning, he saw the little girl standing in the doorway. In an effort to begin forming a bond with her, he'd told her she could watch *Sesame Street*. All kids liked *Sesame Street*. Alice had.

But she'd rejected the suggestion the way she'd rejected everything else so far. He was getting frustrated. The food he'd gotten especially for her still sat on the table, untouched.

Her spirit began to annoy him.

"*Sesame Street* is not on right now, Rachel." He hit the video button on the state-of-the-art set. Nothing but the best for Jackson, he thought sarcastically. A bright-blue screen appeared. He reached into the knapsack he'd brought in from the SUV he'd parked next to the cabin. "I've got a video you might like."

But Rachel continued staring at the blue screen. She'd seen him, seen her father. And heard him say her name. He was looking for her.

"That was my daddy," she announced triumphantly. "He's on TV."

"No, that wasn't your daddy," he said firmly. "Just someone who looked like him." Rachel refused to look at him, staring defiantly at the screen. "I told you, your daddy's gone. He wanted me to take care of you." Taking her arm he yanked once to get her to look at him. "He'd be very sad if he knew you weren't eating. Very sad. You don't want him to be sad, do you?"

Rachel looked over at the table. Her daddy had always said it was important to eat well. He always told her that at breakfast because she didn't like to eat breakfast. Her tummy was always upset when she had to go to school.

Maybe the man was right. Maybe he did know her daddy. Maybe her daddy had told him to take care of her. She didn't know what to think anymore. Her head hurt.

With a sigh Rachel slowly walked toward the table.

The sky that hung over the deep-green rolling fields of the cemetery had turned to a dark shade of gray, as if remaining the bright blue shade it had been early in the morning would somehow be disrespectful to the woman who was being buried today.

The smell of rain was in the air and the only sound that was heard was the voice of the priest who had come from Delia Culhane's parish to officiate over the ceremony.

His head bowed, Brent stood alone by the graveside as the diminutive, older man said a prayer over the gleaming oak coffin. As he listened, Brent couldn't help thinking that it was such a shame that a kindly soul like Delia had no one to mourn for her.

Her end had come too soon. She should have lived a long, full life and when the time finally came for her to leave her earthly home behind, she should have had children, grandchildren and great-grandchildren standing in attendance by her grave.

This wasn't right, it wasn't fair.

A sound caught his attention. Brent turned in time to see Callie approaching. He raised an eyebrow in silent query.

"Sorry I'm late," she apologized in hushed tones. She'd wanted to check out the perimeter herself before joining him. It had taken longer than she'd anticipated. She saw the question in his eyes. He probably thought she was here because they'd discovered something. So far, all the clues they'd been pursuing had led to dead ends. "I thought you might want some company," she explained.

She looked down at the casket, which was the best that the funeral home had to offer. It was a testimony to the judge's character that he'd selected it for his housekeeper. He could just as easily have had her buried in a pine box or cremated, for that matter. No one would have been the wiser.

Callie's regard and respect for Brent Montgomery continued to grow.

Although she'd wanted to be there for him, her appearance at the funeral was not altogether altruistic. A part of her had thought that perhaps the kidnapper might be standing somewhere on the sidelines, drawn out by a morbid curiosity to watch the drama he'd created continue to play itself out.

She had several police officers positioned at various sections of the cemetery. So far there was nothing out of the ordinary to report.

Brent was surprised at how comforting her appearance here was to him. "Thanks."

Making the sign of the cross, the priest ended the service. A kindly smile of condolence on his thin lips, he looked from Callie to Brent. "Anything you would like to say or add?"

Brent wasn't good at personal moments like this. Had trouble speaking what was in his heart. But there was no one to speak for Delia and she had died in his employ, no doubt trying to save his child. He owed her more than he could ever repay.

Brent stepped forward, placing a single white rose on the coffin's lid. "I'm sorry this happened, Delia. Rachel is going to miss you a great deal. You were very good to her, and neither one of us is ever going to forget you."

Callie saw the tears in his eyes then, just a glimmer before he forced them back.

Moved, she slipped her hand into his without thinking, and squeezed. "We're going to find her."

"How?" he demanded once they turned away from the grave and were walking toward his car. The ceremony had gotten to him and for a moment, he was overwhelmed by a feeling of futility. "How are we going to find her? It's been two days, and all we know is that the kidnapper may or may not have been driving a Mercedes."

"He was," she told him quietly, undercutting his tone. "Specifically, because of the impression and a partial tire skid, we know it was a Mercedes 500 SL."

He supposed that was something, although he still felt the information was a long way off from helping them find the kidnapper. "Has anyone reported having their Mercedes stolen?"

"Five people. We're checking their stories out right now. Meanwhile, I have someone getting in contact with the DMV for the names of all Mercedes 500 SL owners in Aurora and the surrounding vicinity. In addition, calls have been pouring in from all over ever since your press conference yesterday, people claiming to have seen Rachel after the kidnapping." The sightings had been from as close as a mile from the site of the abduction to as far away as Santa Fe, New Mexico. Each call was logged and a flag was inserted in a map to mark each site. "We're checking out as many as we can as quickly as we can."

He thought of yesterday morning and the files Callie had taken home with her. "What about the people I put away?"

"We're working on that, too." Her cell phone rang, instantly silencing them both as the sound sliced through the late-morning air. "Cavanaugh." She listened a second, then nodded as she muttered, "Thanks." Shutting the phone, she pushed it back into her jacket pocket. "That was just the police officer I left in charge on the grounds here. No one out of the ordinary has been seen anywhere in the area."

"You thought the kidnapper would come to the funeral?"

"I think the kidnapper wants to see you squirm, wants to see you vulnerable. Funerals have a way of dragging out emotions from the people involved."

She'd certainly seen emotion in his eyes as he'd said his final words over the Culhane woman's coffin. Looking at him, Callie debated for a moment, then asked, "Do you want to go somewhere for a cup of coffee?"

The personal invitation was unexpected and caught him off guard. "Don't you have clues to run down?"

She wondered if he thought she was shirking her responsibility. Nothing could be further from the truth. She considered his well-being a part of her job.

"I have a great team for that. I thought maybe you needed someone to talk to for a few minutes. Someone who qualifies as a sympathetic stranger." She knew how hard it was at times to talk to someone close to you, no matter how well meaning they were. She thought that was why people struck up conversations with total strangers, the need to unburden themselves anonymously.

For a moment that night at the fund-raiser flashed through his mind. "You're not a stranger, Callie."

"Almost," she pointed out. "You don't know anything about me." She noticed that he was looking at her waist. Glancing down, she realized that the hilt of her service revolver was peeking out from beneath her jacket. "Other than the obvious, of course."

He was about to refuse her offer when he thought of returning home. His sister and brother-in-law were still there, waiting to offer comfort at every turn. Fairly or not, he still wasn't in the mood to deal with his sister hovering over him, trying to cheer him up.

And if he was with Callie, he'd be on the front

lines if anything broke. It was what he'd wanted all along. "Coffee sounds good."

"Okay, I know a good place. Why don't we take my car?" she suggested.

He was about to get in on the passenger side when his cell phone rang. It was probably his sister, checking on him, he thought. Childless, she thought of Rachel as her own. The kidnapping had hit her pretty hard, he thought, a flash of guilt traveling through him.

He held up his hand. "Just a second," he said to Callie. Drawing the phone out, he placed it against his ear. "Hello?"

"How does it feel, Judge? How does it feel to lose your daughter?"

Every nerve ending stood at attention. There was no point in trying to recognize the voice on the other end. The caller used one of those synthesizers that distorted voices. Brent could have been talking to a man or a woman for all he knew.

"Where is she, you scum?"

Callie had rounded the hood and was at his side immediately.

"Where is she?" Brent demanded again. "Tell me what you've done with my daughter." The silence mocked him. "If you hurt her, if you so much as harm one of the hairs on Rachel's head, there's no place on earth that you'll be safe. I'll find you and kill you. I swear I will kill you."

"She's mine now."

The scratchy sound of laughter echoed against his ear. And then the line went dead.

Chapter 8

Callie saw anger take hold of every fiber of Brent's body, and she pitied anyone who ever attempted to face down the judge.

"Was that the kidnapper?"

Hardly hearing her, Brent searched his memory, trying to think who could hate him enough to steal his daughter. Somewhere, in the back of his brain, a chord was struck, but he couldn't make it clear, couldn't bring it into the foreground.

He was vaguely aware of nodding his head in response to her question. And then he felt Callie's hand on his shoulder. He looked at her.

Her eyes seemed to scan his face. "Could you recognize his voice?"

"No." He tried not to allow defeat to seize him as he made the admission and shook his head.

"Whoever it was used one of those electronic distorters. It sounded like a robot."

Frustrated, Callie began with the basics. "What did the voice say?" she wanted to know, then cautioned, "Exactly."

The words were still burning in his brain. "He said, 'How does it feel, Judge? How does it feel to lose your daughter?' And then he said, 'She's mine now.'"

It wasn't much. But maybe it was something. There were so many wrong directions to go off in, she thought. But she couldn't allow that to paralyze her. One of these directions had to be the right one, and there was no way to discover that without pushing forward.

"That almost makes it sound as if there was a tug-of-war over your daughter." She raised her eyes to his face, returning to a familiar path. Most missing children were taken by estranged spouses. "Like a custody battle."

"I already told you, there was no custody battle." Bitterness leaked into his voice. "Unless there's a photo op involved, Jennifer wants no part of being a mother if it entails playing the role for more than an hour."

She still wasn't a hundred percent convinced. "What did your ex-wife have to say when you told her that Rachel was missing?"

He frowned as frustration built on frustration. "I haven't been able to reach her. Jennifer's on vacation somewhere in Nevada. Reno, I think, although I'm really not sure.''

On vacation. Convenient. Callie made a mental note to get in touch with the Reno police and have the woman tracked down. From everything Brent had told her, it sounded as if Jennifer Montgomery had willingly washed her hands of all parental privileges, but you never knew what went on in a person's head. At the very least, the woman might want the child as leverage for reasons of her own.

But for now Callie decided to turn her attention in a different direction. Maybe she'd missed something in reviewing the judge's cases. If there wasn't a tug-of-war over this particular child, maybe the kidnapping signified a tit-for-tat frame of mind. Someone had had their daughter taken away by the judge, so now he was taking away the judge's daughter.

''Was there anyone you convicted of incest, Brent? A father separated from the daughter he was abusing?''

The question seemed to come out of nowhere. He shook his head. ''No, I haven't had any cases like that.'' Damn it, why weren't they making any progress? ''You know that,'' he heard himself snapping. ''You've been through the cases with me.''

Callie sighed. ''Right.'' But there was something nagging at her, something they'd overlooked or skimmed over. Something that had registered on the perimeter of her mind, maybe late that night as she'd been reviewing the cases. Something that she couldn't readily summon now. ''At least now we know that it was a kidnapping with a definite motive.''

''Then why kill Delia?''

That was simple. ''Because she got in the way. Because she could identify the kidnapper.'' Callie stopped as another thought struck her. She saw Brent looking at her expectantly. Hopefully. The slowness of the process was as frustrating to her as it was to him. ''In calling you, it seems as if revenge isn't enough. He wants you to know that this wasn't a random act, that Rachel was not just in the wrong place at the wrong time, but that he specifically chose her. I'm hoping now that his ego will make him want you to know that it's him. That he's the one who caused you all this grief.''

Brent wasn't into subtlety. Black-and-white suited him far better. ''If that's the case, then why didn't he tell me who he was?''

''Because this is a game to him, most likely a game he's waited a long time to play. He wants to draw it out, to enjoy making you suffer.''

Brent gave voice to the one thing that terrified him the most. ''Do you think he's harmed her?''

The look in his eyes begged her for the truth, but also entreated her to make it the right truth. The truth he wanted to hear. That his little girl was all right. To her surprise, Callie realized that she would have lied to him to erase the pain she saw there.

But fortunately she felt she didn't have to. She believed in her theory.

''Other than scared her, no, I don't think he's

harmed her. It's in his best interest to keep your daughter alive so he can taunt you with her.'' She was about to say more when her cell phone rang. Smothering impatience, she flashed an apologetic smile at him. "I don't think we're ever getting out of this parking lot for that cup of coffee," she commented, taking out her phone. "Cavanaugh."

She heard Adams on the other end of the line. "One of the suspects you wanted me to run down is AWOL. John Walker hasn't checked in with his parole officer in a couple of weeks."

Maybe this was finally it. Adrenaline began to pump through her veins. "We have an address for this shy parolee?"

"Last known residence was a motel in one of the city's less-than-stellar areas. Skylight Inn."

A motel. That meant that Walker had at least gotten past a halfway house. But predators had patience, she thought.

"We're not here to judge, Adams, we're here just to track them down." Juggling the cell against her ear and shoulder, she pulled out her pad. "Want to give me the address?" As Adams recited it, she quickly scribbled it down in what her father had once said looked like hieroglyphics. "Got it." She flipped the pad closed. "Good work. I'll take it from here. Keep going down the list."

Adams said something unintelligible as he hung up. Callie figured she was better off not knowing what he'd said. The man was a good detective, just a lousy human being.

Brent was on her the second she closed the cell phone. "What do you have?"

"A possible lead." She tried to recall what she'd gleaned from Walker's file the other day. She couldn't remember if the man had a daughter or not. "John Walker was paroled six months ago. He was a no-show at his last meeting with his parole officer." While wanting to keep his spirits from flagging, she didn't want to raise his hopes up too high, either. "Could be nothing," she warned, telling him what she figured he already knew. "A lot of ex-cons pull disappearing acts." There was a more important question to ask. "Do you remember him displaying any particular sense of hostility toward you when they took him away?"

Brent was quiet for a moment, trying to recall the case, the mood that had surrounded the trial. Only vague facts returned to him. He doubted even those would have returned if he and Callie hadn't spent so much time going over his cases.

Walker was a two-bit junkie who had robbed a liquor store owner of the princely sum of sixty-three dollars while waving a realistic looking toy gun. It had been his second offense. Brent could remember no remorse being displayed. "No more than usual. He was angrier at his lawyer for not getting him off because he'd used a toy gun instead of the real thing than he was at me. I don't think I really entered into the picture for him."

Maybe yes, maybe no. Maybe Rachel represented freedom rather than a child to the man. Brent took away his freedom, he was going to take away something precious from the judge.

"Still, I have to check it out."

Brent nodded, eager to stop talking and start doing. "I want to come with you."

"And I want you to come with me." Too late, she realized how that must sound to him. Why had she worded it that way? she berated herself silently. "The kidnapper might call you back. I want to know the second he does. Best way I know to do that is to keep you around as much as possible." She led the way to her car. It went without saying that they would use hers and return later for his. "Just as long as you remember to stay out of the way if anything goes down," she warned. "The last thing either one of us needs is for you to get shot."

He stopped at her vehicle. "But you getting shot is okay?"

The corner of her mouth curved upward. "Never okay. I've just had more training at covering my tail than you have."

"No," he agreed wryly, his eyes traveling to that portion of her anatomy almost against his will, "they never went over tail covering in judge school."

She heard the note of cynicism in his voice. "I meant no disrespect."

Brent sighed. He supposed no one ever knew how they would react under dire circumstances until they occurred. He really was going to have to get better control over himself than this. "Neither did I. It's

NO POSTAGE
NECESSARY
IF MAILED
IN THE
UNITED STATES

BUSINESS REPLY MAIL

FIRST-CLASS MAIL   PERMIT NO. 717-003   BUFFALO, NY

POSTAGE WILL BE PAID BY ADDRESSEE

SILHOUETTE READER SERVICE
3010 WALDEN AVE
PO BOX 1867
BUFFALO NY 14240-9952

Do You
Have the
LUCKY
KEY?

PLAY THE
Lucky Key Game

and you can get

FREE BOOKS
and a FREE GIFT!

Scratch
the gold
areas with a
coin. Then check
below to see the
books and
gift you can get!

YES!
I have scratched off the gold areas. Please send me
the **2 FREE BOOKS** and **GIFT** for which I qualify.
I understand I am under no obligation to purchase
any books, as explained on the back of this card.

345 SDL DVAG   245 SDL DVAW

FIRST NAME   LAST NAME

ADDRESS

APT.#   CITY

STATE/PROV.   ZIP/POSTAL CODE

🔑🔑🔑🔑 2 free books plus a free gift   🔑🔑 1 free book

🔑🔑🔑 2 free books   Try Again!

Visit us online at
www.eHarlequin.com

DETACH AND MAIL CARD TODAY!

(S-IM-10/03)

© 2002 HARLEQUIN ENTERPRISES LTD. ® and ™ are
trademarks owned by Harlequin Books, S.A. used under license.

just that my nerves are stretched further than I ever thought was possible.''

Without thinking, she laid a hand on his shoulder. ''You're doing fine.''

The soft note in Callie's voice unlocked something within him. Brent looked at her hand, grateful for the comfort, wary that there was something more happening here than either one of them could allow at the moment. Something that, once this was brought to a successful end, perhaps could be examined more closely. But not here, not now.

Suddenly becoming aware of the contact, Callie dropped her hand. ''We'd better go.''

With that, she rounded the hood of her car and got in on the driver's side. If her heart was beating just a little harder than it should have been, she attributed it to the rush of adrenaline associated with chasing down a possible lead.

John Walker didn't answer his door when she knocked. Laying her ear against the door, she heard no movement on the other side. There was no reason to believe that the man was there.

But, if he was their man, maybe he'd left behind a clue, something for them to go on.

''You stay here,'' she told Brent in case the ex-con actually was inside and playing possum. ''I'm going to get the motel manager. If Walker does happen to turn up, I want you to come get me. Nothing else, understand?''

It took no subtle reading of body language to know

that the instruction annoyed the hell out of him. "I'm not a child, Callie."

"You're not bulletproof, either. I'll be right back."

She hurried away, hoping this wouldn't take too long. The manager was in his small, crammed office. The smell of years of grime mingled with stale body odor the moment she opened the door.

Callie flashed her ID at him. The bald, mousy-looking man squinted at it as if he was trying to make out the letters.

"You have a John Walker staying in room 212. He's not answering and I have reason to suspect he might be holding a child prisoner inside. I need you to open the door for me."

With two hands on the counter, the manager seemed to hold the narrow separation as an obstacle between him and her. "I can't do that. That's a violation of his civil rights."

It sounded as if a lawyer had been whispering in the man's ear. Obviously, the motel had had more than one unsavory character staying here lately. "We'll discuss civil rights on our way to the room." Callie left no room for argument in her voice.

The manager complained and whined all the way to the second-floor door, then he stood stubbornly before the door, making no move to open it. Callie glanced at Brent, but the man shook his head. Walker hadn't made an appearance one way or another.

"When did you last see Walker?" Callie asked the manager.

The man raised what little chin he had defiantly. "Dunno. A week, two. They pay, I don't bother them." He peered myopically at Callie. "Look, you sure this is legal? I don't want to get in no trouble here. Already had lawyers coming at me and I don't particularly like the experience."

Brent moved in front of Callie. "I'm Judge Brenton Montgomery."

The manager's eyes widened as he looked at Callie. "You brought your judge?"

"I've issued a search warrant for the premises," Brent told him. "This man could be involved in a kidnapping case. If you don't want to be charged with obstructing justice, I suggest you open the door immediately."

The manager couldn't find the proper key quickly enough. Hands trembling, he inserted it into the lock.

"I didn't know judges were allowed to lie," Callie whispered to Brent under her breath.

Brent kept his eyes on the door as the manager struggled with the lock.

"I didn't lie," he whispered back. "I am a judge, and we already know that Walker could be involved in the case."

It was nice to know Brent was human like the rest of them, she thought. "I was talking about the warrant."

He moved the manager out of the way and took hold of the key, turning it. "Just getting a little ahead of myself."

They both knew he could issue one on the spot if

there was reason enough to suspect that Walker was somehow involved in Rachel's abduction. He put his shoulder to the door and shoved it opened.

The smell that hit Callie the instant the door was opened was sadly familiar. She was grateful that she'd put some time between herself and the breakfast she'd had at her father's house. Even so, she could feel it threatening to make a reappearance.

John Walker was lying sprawled out on the floor by the window. The right side of his head was bashed opened.

She wasn't one of those people who could get accustomed or hardened to the sight of a murder victim, even though it was all part of her job. It didn't matter that the man on the floor had probably been a man no one had ever cared about, much less loved. Who, according to his file, was an incorrigible criminal. No one deserved to die like this. No one deserved to rot in a room for several days, their disappearance from life unnoticed.

"Damn," she heard Brent say.

"That would be the word for it," she murmured.

Reaching into her pocket, Callie took out the gloves that were part and parcel of her job and slipped them on before she began examining the body.

Brent had to shove his hands into his pockets to keep from giving in to the urge to help with the search. "Is he— Is he—?"

"Dead?" Though she knew it was futile, she felt for a pulse in Walker's neck. There was none. The man's color was gone. He'd bled out. "Very much so." She glanced up at the manager, who looked as if he was going to be sick right on the spot. "I hope he paid for the room in advance, because he's sure as hell not going to be making any payments now."

Taking care to keep out of her way, Brent squatted down beside Callie. "Do you think he was involved in Rachel's kidnapping?"

Her very first case had involved a man who'd been dead a little more than a day. Walker was stiffer than that man had been.

"If he was, I'd say it was way before the actual fact." Holding up Walker's hand she tested its flexibility. There was none. "Judging from the rigor that's set in, not to mention the smell, this man has been dead for about three or four days. He certainly wasn't the one who just placed that call to you, or snatched up your daughter." Her stomach inching its way into her throat, Callie rose to her feet and stepped back. She automatically dug out her cell phone as she turned from the body. "We'll know more once the CSI team gets here."

Brent looked down at her. The blood had drained from her face. "You all right?"

"I'm not at my best around dead people. Thanks for noticing."

The words sounded sarcastic. The smile of thanks she offered was not.

It was another frustrating dead end.

Callie frowned, hating to have her back against the

wall. Again. It had taken very little investigating to discover that this was just a drug score gone bad. The dealer had taken Walker's money and left with the stash he had come to pedal. The whole thing was completely unrelated to Rachel Montgomery's kidnapping case.

They weren't getting anywhere with the other suspects on the list, either. So far, all had alibis that were holding up under investigation. She was beginning to wonder if perhaps this *was* a clumsy random snatch and someone was just using it to taunt the Judge.

She kept this latest theory to herself, not wanting to add to Brent's agitation.

He'd been with her for the duration of the day, offering suggestions but mostly waiting. Waiting for a break. Waiting to get his life back in order. She felt as if she was failing him.

It was an odd feeling. No matter how caught up she got in a case, she'd never felt it as personally as she did this one. Having him with her didn't help, she thought. But she would have felt inordinately cruel, asking him to stay home to carry out his vigil on his own.

They were back at the cemetery where they had originally gotten hooked up this morning. Her thought was to get him back to his car and call it a night, but now that she was here, she couldn't quite make herself slip quietly into the darkness.

Pulling up the hand brake, she looked at Brent. If

his square jaw was any more clenched, she was certain it was in danger of shattering.

"Look, it's getting late, why don't I follow you to your house? I could make you something to eat. You haven't eaten anything all day."

As if to agree with her, his stomach growled. He laughed shortly, but there was little humor evident in his eyes. "You haven't eaten, either."

"All right, I'll make something for both of us. I figure you're probably too tired to be very critical. I'm not my father."

Desperate to have something to think about rather than dwell on the obvious, he picked up the thread of her conversation.

"Very few people can cook the way he can," Brent agreed. "I'm surprised he never opened up a restaurant after he retired."

"I think he likes being exclusive." She tried to remember ever seeing Brent at their table and failed. It had to have been for one of those dinners she'd missed, she decided. But she was curious. "When did you have my father's cooking?"

He shook his head as he looked around. The cemetery was peaceful. It only added to his sense of agitation. *Where was she?* "I haven't. But I've heard Judge Morehead talking about attending one of your father's cook-outs."

She smiled. "Dad likes to keep abreast of what's going on. Inviting all his old friends and their families does that for him. He usually winds up playing host to half the Aurora police force. He cooks, they talk, everyone ends up happy.''

Brent nodded, only half listening. What made a woman like her get into this line of work, he wondered. A line of work that involved unsolved cases and staring down at dead people. What did she do with her nights to cleanse herself? To get herself to sound this bright, this chipper? This hopeful.

He realized that she'd stopped talking, and he dug the conversation back from the borders of his mind. ''Must get expensive.''

''Not so bad,'' she contradicted. ''Besides, that kind of thing is priceless for him.'' She nodded toward his car. They should get going. She hadn't believed in creatures that went bump in the night since she was a little girl, but that didn't mean she liked standing around at the gates of a cemetery at night with a fog encroaching. ''Why don't you get into your car and I'll follow you home?'' she repeated. Her words played themselves back to her. She was being pushy, she realized. As usual. She gave him a way out. ''Unless you want to be alone.''

Aiming his key ring at the car, Brent pressed down. Two short noises signaled that the alarm was disarmed, the car unlocked. Brent shook his head. ''No, I don't want to be alone.''

Callie didn't realize she was smiling until she caught her own reflection in the side mirror as she got into her own vehicle.

The ground floor of Brent's house was spacious, airy. If his wife had done any decorating here, there was precious little evidence of it now. The furnishings were decidedly masculine. Massive pieces chosen for comfort rather than for elegance.

She followed him to a kitchen her father would have approved of. It had a great deal of counter space and looked out onto a family room that was built around a giant projection screen. Her own apartment could have fit into one of the corners of the room.

"Make yourself at home." Brent indicated the giant built-in refrigerator. "Use whatever you need, although I have to tell you, I'm not hungry."

"You have to eat. You have to keep up your strength." My God, she sounded just like her father whenever she protested that she didn't feel like eating. With a shake of her head, Callie opened the refrigerator. She was going to have to watch that.

Unlike her own, this refrigerator was almost fully stocked. Delia must have gone shopping just before she was killed, she thought. Callie decided on something simple. "How do you feel about an omelet?"

Brent had walked into the family room. Picking up the remote, he aimed it at the set.

"That'll be fine."

As had been his habit since he'd been in college, he turned on the television set to see what else had been going on in the world. Without looking, he moved his thumb from TV to cable mode and pressed a button. Instead of the all-news channel he expected, he heard the sound of childish laughter.

The screen flickered. The next moment, the image of his daughter appeared. She was at someone's birthday party. He'd accidentally hit the VCR mode instead of the auxiliary cable.

His heart froze.

Callie's head jerked up the moment she heard the laughter. She moved away from the stove as she heard a high voice cry out, "Watch me, Daddy, watch me!"

He hadn't meant to play this, she realized. Most likely, the tape had been in the machine all this time. That first night Rachel had been kidnapped, had Brent stayed up looking at videotapes of his little girl?

Leaving the kitchen, she crossed to Brent. For a moment she stood beside him, watching the child on the screen. "She's a beautiful little girl."

He felt as if his throat was constricting again. His eyes stung, and this time he didn't bother trying to blink back the tears. Would he ever see her again?

"Yes, she is," he agreed quietly. His fingers tightened around the remote, but he made no move to stop the video. "I shouldn't be standing here, doing nothing. Thinking about eating. Thinking about—" His voice halted as guilt abruptly washed over his face.

"Thinking about what?" Callie half expected him to say something about killing the man who'd done this horrible thing.

She was caught completely by surprise when he quietly confessed, "You."

Chapter 9

Brent wasn't sure if he made the first move, or if Callie did.

It didn't matter.

All he was aware of was the incredible need he had to make human contact, to find comfort and somehow lessen this pain he was feeling. Make it fade for just a moment.

There had been something humming between them all along. It had been there since that first moment at the fund-raiser when he'd seen her from across the room and asked for her name.

It urged him on now, playing upon this awful vulnerability he felt.

Cupping the back of her head, he turned her face up to his. Brought his lips down to hers.

The moment froze in time.

For a second Callie didn't know what to think, how to react. And then her arms were around his neck and she was leaning into the kiss. Giving him comfort. Taking the same away for herself.

She'd been so alone since Kyle had been killed, alone in that secret place in her heart that he had brought to life. That place where love had existed. After Kyle was killed, it had felt like a barren wasteland. Until this moment.

Brent took her breath away and with it the thoughts that always lingered on the outskirts of her mind, haunting her. They all burned away in the heat of the kiss as it traveled up and down the length of her body, taking the shell of the woman she once was and recreating her.

Callie felt herself surrendering without a single shot being fired, before a single line of defense had the opportunity to be set up.

The kiss grew in intensity, in demand. She melted with it.

When he'd been in college and on the boxing team, there'd been a term for this. Sucker punched. He'd just been sucker punched, trying so hard to hold his line of defense in place, he'd never seen this coming.

And had taken it squarely on the chin. It sent him reeling.

His senses on fire, Brent slipped his arms down to her waist, and he drew her closer to him. Drew her warmth, her comfort, into him. He would have absorbed her completely if he could.

And then his mind went on the alert.

Damn it, what was he thinking, what was he doing? His baby was out there somewhere, needing him, and he was standing in his family room, with a video of Rachel flickering in the background, kissing the woman in charge of finding her.

Like a shell-shocked soldier, Brent drew back, shaken and in disbelief over what had just happened. "I'm sorry, I didn't—"

She knew what was coming, inexplicably privy to his thoughts. Callie placed her finger against his lips, stopping the flow of words.

"Shh. There's nothing to apologize for." She took a breath to steady her own nerves and found that it really didn't help. All she had was honesty. "This kiss was a long time in coming." Her eyes held his, the memory of the dance they had once shared firmly in place for all time. Taking another breath, she turned back to the kitchen. "The omelet's coming along. How do you feel about red peppers?"

It took him a second to come around. He felt as if everything inside of him vibrated like a tuning fork. "What?"

"In your omelet, how do you feel about red peppers?" Callie tried very hard to sound unaffected. As if she hadn't just crossed over into another time zone entirely. As if that kiss hadn't shaken something loose.

His stomach was the least of his concerns. Crossing to the television set, Brent waved a dismissive hand at the question.

"All right, I guess. Detective—" He wanted to regain ground, but you couldn't call the woman you'd just kissed by some formal title the city had awarded her. Stopping the videotape, he closed the television set and tried again. "Callie—I had no business kissing you."

She offered him a tenuous smile, then turned away to the stove. "That had nothing to do with business. That was about one human being comforting another."

He blew out a breath. This one was steadier. "Is that what it was, you were comforting me?"

She looked at him over her shoulder, an enigmatic smile playing along her lips. "I said human being, I didn't say who was doing the comforting. Why don't you go wash up? This'll be ready soon." She saw the smallest hint of a smile bloom on his face and then spread out. "What?"

"The last time someone told me to wash up, I was eight. It was the maid," he tagged on, delineating how different his home life had been from hers when he had been growing up.

She grabbed at the innocuous topic with both hands, grateful for its appearance. "Then it's high time you followed the rules of proper hygiene. By the time you finish, I should have your serving ready. Now go." Callie waved him on with the edge of her spatula.

When he'd returned from the bathroom, the omelet was waiting for him. Taking his seat, he knew he should have felt ill-at-ease or at least awkward in her presence because of the momentary lapse in his control.

But he didn't feel awkward, didn't feel as if he was tottering on a cliff, about to make a fatal misstep. Instead, there was something about Callie Cavanaugh that put him at his ease, even after kissing her without any preamble. He'd felt it right from the start. At the fund-raiser. Felt the electricity crackling between them despite the fact that he had never seen her before. Despite the fact that he was struggling to keep his marriage alive and together.

Electricity. The same kind that was crackling between them now, despite the dire situation that existed in his life.

He took another forkful, allowing himself to savor the taste before asking, ''So, what do we do now?''

Callie had almost finished her own portion. Her stomach in an uproar, she'd sought to appease it even though she really wasn't hungry. The cheese omelet seemed to settle it as much as it could be settled, given the circumstances.

''About the case?'' Afraid he was referring to what had just happened between them, she didn't want to give him the opportunity to respond and jumped in with a reply. ''We continue chasing down leads.'' She'd checked in with Ramon Diaz, one of her men, for a progress report just before Brent had walked in. ''There's no shortage of those. At last count we've logged in something like eight thousand phone calls and there's no end in sight.'' She did her best to sound upbeat as she told him, ''All the callers are certain they saw your little girl. And my team still hasn't finished checking out those people on your list. There are several more names to go.''

What if none of them had her? What if they all checked out clean? What then? He looked at her. ''And after that?''

Checking out the phone calls would keep them busy. But she was hoping they'd have their answer before that happened. ''One step at a time, Brent, we take it one step at a time.''

Impatient, restless, he pushed his plate away. ''Time. Isn't that what we're running out of?'' He gave voice to what had been haunting him with each passing hour. ''I heard that if you don't find a child within the first thirty-six hours...'' Choked with emotion, his voice trailed off.

''It's not a hard-and-fast rule, Brent.'' She slipped her hand over his. ''We're doing everything we can. Every available police officer has been put on this. Vacations have been canceled. Nobody's taking any time off. We *will* find her.''

The smile on his lips was so sad, it tore at her heart. ''You must be getting tired of telling me that.''

''I'll say it as often as you want me to.'' She gave his hand a firm squeeze and with it, a silent promise. ''Because it's true.''

He nodded. He knew she meant what she said and he had to believe it was true. Resigned, trying to make the best of it, Brent drew the plate toward him and forced himself to take another bite of the omelet. Until he'd begun eating, he hadn't realized that he was actually hungry. His stomach rallied around the offering, reminding him that it was still pinched.

He felt her watching him and raised his eyes to hers. "This is good."

Callie grinned. "Of course it's good. I learned from the best." She saw him about to lay down his fork again. "Less talking, more eating," she urged.

"Yes, ma'am."

He watched her sleep. When she had her hand tucked under her cheek like that, she looked just like Alice. His Alice used to sleep that way.

He felt his heart swelling as he sat down beside her. The little girl looked dwarfed in the double bed. It was only temporary. When he got his bearings, he'd get her a better bed. Her own bed.

Very gently he brushed away the hair that had fallen into her face. She stirred, and he immediately withdrew his hand, freezing his motion, his very breath. He didn't want to risk waking her. It had taken her a while to drop off to sleep. But it was better than yesterday. Which had been better than the night before.

She was getting used to him.

He wondered how she would react to being called Alice. It was a far better name than Rachel.

Alice.

It suited her.

Cocking his head, he continued to stare at her small, innocent face. If he tried real hard, he could almost believe that this was his Alice. She had the same blond hair, the same round face. She was even the same age as he remembered.

His Alice.

His mouth curved in a satisfied smile, seeing the humor in the situation. The judge taketh away and the judge giveth. Not willingly, of course, but that didn't count. The only thing that counted was that he had his daughter back. Finally.

The sound of the phone ringing bore into Brent's brain, startling him awake. He was grabbing both sides of the armchair, braced, before he was fully conscious. He tried to focus.

He couldn't remember falling asleep after Callie had left. He'd sat down in the chair to try to think, and exhaustion had gotten the better of him. It fled now as he grabbed the telephone, hoping it was the kidnapper. "Hello?"

There was no formality, no greeting, the female voice on the other end of the line went straight for the attack. "I just had two of Reno's so-called 'finest' banging on my hotel room door like I was some common call girl. Why didn't you tell me?"

Jennifer. Nothing had changed, he thought, scrubbing his hand over his face, trying to pull together his senses. The sound of her voice, once so melodious to his ear, only grated on his nerves now. "I've been trying to reach you for the past three days." He wanted to ask her where the hell she'd been for that time, but it really didn't matter. Having Jennifer close by wouldn't have helped to bring Rachel back.

"Well, these two burly cops could certainly 'reach' me," she huffed. "They told me some idiot named Detective Cavanaugh wants to see me for questioning. What the hell happened?"

He felt the hairs on the back of his neck rising at her tone, especially the way she spoke of Callie. But he wasn't up to getting embroiled in another shouting match with Jennifer. He'd vowed the last time around that there would be no more, that he didn't care enough about her to unleash his emotions again. But this wasn't about her, it was about Rachel, and he could feel his control thinning.

As succinctly as he could, he gave her the highlights of the past three days.

"And there's no other news?" she demanded.

He couldn't get a handle on whether she was actually genuinely concerned or she wanted to know what kind of clothes to wear for the occasion. Black for mourning, red for hope.

How could he have ever fallen in love with someone so shallow, so transparent?

"None."

He heard her huff in his ear again. "How could this have happened? What kind of nanny did you get for our daughter?"

Our daughter. She'd never been that, not from the moment of conception. Rachel had always been his. He'd saved her life before she ever drew her first breath. And somehow, some way, he was going to save it again.

Taking umbrage in defense of Delia, he snapped,

"The best, Jennifer. The woman gave up her life trying to save Rachel."

Jennifer snorted disparagingly. "How do you know that?"

He nearly lost it then. "She's dead, Jennifer, that's proof enough for me."

"I don't have time to argue with you," she announced. "I've got to pack. I'm getting the first plane to Aurora in the morning."

He glanced at his watch. It was almost eleven. Flights left almost every hour. In her situation he would have grabbed the first flight he could get on. Chartered a plane if he had to. But Jennifer liked to make entrances, and there would be more reporters around in the daytime. More people around to see the grieving mother disembark. He had no doubt that she was probably on the phone with someone from *Gentry Magazine,* making sure there would be a photographer alerted as to which flight she was arriving on. It had taken him four years to finally admit to himself that everything was always about her.

"There's nothing you can do, Jennifer."

There was indignation in her voice as she retorted, "I'm her mother. I should be there."

She didn't sound very convincing, but maybe he was just feeling more jaded than usual. The hour was late and he didn't feel like being charitable. He was operating on overload as it was.

"Fine, suit yourself."

He could tell by her tone that it wasn't what she

wanted to hear. But the days of trying to appease her were long behind him.

''I'll call you in the morning with my flight number,'' she informed him icily. ''You can meet me.''

He was right. She was angling for a photo op. ''I'm going to be too busy trying to find Rachel, Jennifer. You can take a cab from the airport. On me.''

She snapped at him, saying something disparaging about his lineage. He had no energy to take offense. More likely than not, there was probably a kernel of truth in it, he thought. He heard a loud bang on the other end before the line went dead.

Brent shook his head as he replaced the receiver. To think that he had once given his heart to that woman. How could he feel so certain, so clear-headed on the bench and make such a terrible misjudgment in his personal life? It made a man doubt himself.

But then, if he hadn't married Jennifer, he would never have had Rachel in his life. And she, he reminded himself, was worth anything he had to go through.

He reached for the remote he'd dropped on the coffee table earlier and turned on the TV. This time he deliberately hit the video play button.

''Why aren't you home, in bed?''

Poring over the notes in her pad, Callie was oblivious to her surroundings. At the sound of his voice, she looked up in time to see her father walking toward her in the darkened squad room.

Most of the others on the task force had long since left for the night, exhausted by their efforts.

They were all exhausted, she thought. But there was no time to take a breather. She'd breathe after Rachel was recovered.

She'd been here for the past four hours, after leaving Brent's house. The look on his face would have made going home and to bed impossible.

She'd had one piece of good news since she'd come in. The Reno police had called to say that Jennifer Montgomery had been located and was coming into the precinct sometime after eight.

Probably closer to noon if she knew her socialites, Callie thought.

She pushed back a little from her desk to look up at her father. "What are you doing here, Dad? Come to give me some expert advise?"

His eyes washed over her. They didn't like what they saw. She looked tired with a capital *T*. "Yes, don't kill the goose that lays the golden egg."

She scrubbed her hands over her face and leaned back in her chair. It squeaked. "Maybe it's the hour, but I didn't quite get that."

"Then I'll make it simple for you." Hand on the top of her chair, he leaned over until his face was level with hers. "Go home, Callie Rose. Go home and get some rest or you won't be any good to anyone."

She laughed, shaking her head. "This from a man who used to pull double shifts."

His expression told her she'd just underscored his point. "Exactly. I know of what I speak."

She leaned her head back to relieve the tension and heard her neck crack softly. She felt as if she'd been sitting there close to forever. But if Jennifer was coming in, she wanted to be ready for her. No one had to tell her that the woman was going to require kid-glove handling.

Callie smiled as she looked up at her father. "Did you come in specifically to harass me?"

He straightened. Closer to sixty than fifty, he still had the posture of a police academy cadet. "It's a dirty job, but someone has to do it." He grew serious. "I called your apartment, but you didn't answer. I figured you were here. Working too hard." Protectiveness stirred within him. "You're not going to help the judge find his daughter by falling on your face."

"I'm not falling on my face," she protested good-naturedly, knowing he meant well. "I'm a Cavanaugh. We're indestructible."

He couldn't help laughing. "And who's been feeding you that line of bull?"

She leaned her chin on her upturned palm and fluttered her lashes at him. "You. All my life."

He narrowed his eyes. "I never said you were indestructible."

"No," she agreed. "You said you were. I just

figured I had your genes. Ergo, if A equals B and B equals C, then A equals C.''

Andrew snorted, waving a hand at her reasoning. ''I don't know anything about any 'ergo' and you know damn well that I was never any good at solving math problems.'' That had always been Rose's field of expertise. That was why he'd handed over the bank book and other matters of finance to her. Losing her had shaken up everything in his life down to the smallest detail.

''No, only crimes,'' Callie said cheerfully, affection resonating in her voice. Pride joined it as she added, ''Best record in the business.''

''Except where it counted.'' As far as he was concerned, his wife's case was still open, still unsolved. He'd solved hundreds of cases during his days on the force, and yet the one that mattered most to him, he'd never been able to close to his satisfaction.

He refused to believe, like his brothers and the other members of the force had, that Rose was dead. You couldn't kill anyone with that much life in them, you just couldn't.

Pushing the topic out of his mind for the moment, Andrew crossed over to the bulletin board. There was a great deal of writing on it now, not to mention photographs and scraps of information. The map that was adjacent to it had a myriad of white pushpins in it, each designating another Rachel sighting.

Which were real?

There was sympathy in his eyes as he turned to look at his daughter. He knew exactly what Brent had to be going through. Knew every jagged inch of the shard-covered path. "So, how's it going?"

She rose and came up to stand beside him. "We're not making any headway."

He nodded at the information. His voice was almost too innocent as he asked, "Do you think you might make some in the next couple of hours?"

"No." And then she stopped and laughed at herself. "Fell right into that one, didn't I?"

There was pleasure in his laugh. "Don't feel bad. I'm craftier than you are."

She wasn't about to concede without at least a pretense of a fight. "I'm just tired."

Andrew nodded. "My point exactly. Come home, Callie," he urged softly. "Get a good night's sleep. Maybe you'll come up with something tomorrow."

He was lying, but she needed to hear that. Needed to pretend that it was true. "You think so?"

Andrew inclined his head, his eyes softening as he looked at her. "Hope, Callie." He slipped his arm around her shoulder, gently prodding her toward the exit. "That's all any of us ever has. Hope."

She let herself be led. "You're a stubborn old man, you know that?"

"So I've been told." He flipped off the light switch, leaving only the emergency lights on. "Can I expect you for breakfast tomorrow?"

They were walking toward the elevator. She almost gave in to the impulse to lean her head against his shoulder, the way she used to when she was younger and needed to feel his strength.

"Do I have a choice?"

"No."

"Then you can expect me."

"Good." He leaned over and pressed for the elevator. "I was hoping you'd say that." And then he surprised her by kissing her forehead.

"What was that for?"

Brent's tragedy brought home to him just how lucky a man he was. All of his children were accounted for. "Just counting my blessings, Callie. Just counting my blessings."

Chapter 10

The doorbell rang just as she was putting on her holster. Muttering under her breath, Callie slipped on her jacket and hurried to the door. She hadn't the slightest idea who would be standing on the other side this early. It was barely seven.

She said "Yes?" as she opened it.

The last person in the world she expected to see was there on the second-floor landing, framed in the hazy morning light. The dampness in the air curled the ends of his black hair. He didn't look like a criminal court judge, just a very sensual man.

"How did you get my address?"

"There are certain privileges that go along with being a judge." He frowned disapprovingly. "You have no peephole."

She felt that inexplicable "something" coming to

life within her. The same something that sent her blood flowing through her veins just a tad faster than it had been. Than it should be.

Callie shrugged, hoping he couldn't read anything in her face. "The apartment didn't come with one."

That was no excuse. She was a young, attractive woman living alone. That meant she needed all the edge she could get to hold her own in the city. He didn't like the fact that she was lax with her own safety. "Don't you even ask who's there? You're a detective, shouldn't you know better?"

"I'm a detective," she echoed. "That means I can protect myself." Callie opened the door wider to allow him entrance, then turned and walked away. She needed to finish getting ready. "What are you doing here, if you don't mind my asking?" She'd expected him to be at the precinct, not here.

He'd asked himself the same question as he'd pulled up to her apartment complex. There had been no real answer to that. He was here because he needed to be here. "I thought I could take you to work."

Throwing a roll of mints into her small, utilitarian purse, she looked up at him. "I need my car."

He lifted a single shoulder carelessly. "Then you can take me." Brent sighed. The truth didn't come easily for him. Not when it was about him, and personal. But he owed it to her to be honest. "The truth is, I need someone to talk to before I go crazy." He saw the surprised expression on her face. She was going to ask about his sister. He headed her off.

"Someone professional who won't just pat my hand and feed me empty platitudes."

Callie closed the flap on her purse. "I'm not going straight to work."

He didn't care where she was going, just as long as she talked to him. Made him feel by her very competent presence that this was going to come to a satisfactory conclusion instead of the one that haunted him every time he was alone with his thoughts. "Do whatever you usually do. I just need the human contact."

He needed to be kept busy. Too busy to think. "Have you thought about going back to work?"

"I've thought about it," he replied. However, his integrity wouldn't allow him to use his position on the bench as a way to block out his thoughts. "But in my present preoccupied state, I wouldn't be doing the state or the course of justice any service by presiding over cases." He watched her take out her keys. "Where do you have to go first?"

She stopped at the front door and looked at him, wondering how he'd react to knowing that she still made it a point to see her father almost every day. Without realizing it, she raised her chin in a movement of defiance.

"I usually stop by my father's house before going in to work. He makes breakfast for the clan. It gives him a sense of purpose, of unity." She realized she sounded defensive and did her best to tone it down. "I guess it gives all of us a sense of unity."

The idea was completely foreign to him. When he

was growing up, he couldn't wait until he didn't have to look at his parents across any table. "How many of you are there?"

"Any given morning?" She did a quick calculation, then laughed. "A crowd. He likes to have my brothers, my sisters and me there as often as possible. And sometimes our cousins and uncle pop up."

A family affair. Maybe he'd just go on to the precinct and hook up with her later. "Then I'd be intruding."

"You didn't let me mention assorted friends," Callie pointed out. "My father sets a very large table. The more seats, the better."

Brent figured that as a retired police chief her father's pension was a sizable one. Still, feeding a lot of people on a regular basis had to take a large chunk of change out of it. "That sort of thing must get expensive."

She waited for him to walk out, then followed, locking the door behind them. "Not if you count it in terms of warmth. Then it's priceless." Hunting up her car keys on the ring, she smiled at Brent. "Now that I think of it, you could benefit from a trip to the House of Cavanaugh."

He resisted the urge to take her arm, helping her down the stairs. This wasn't a date, he reminded himself, no matter how attracted he was to her or how comfortable she made him feel. Instead he followed her down the wooden steps.

"Is that anything like the House of Pancakes?"

Reaching the bottom, she turned to look up at him.

"I doubt if anyone at the House of Pancakes would take you to task for being late." With that she led the way to space 189 and her car.

He had his doubts about barging in.

Pulling up at the curb in front of the pleasant-looking two-story stucco structure, Brent was beginning to have second thoughts about sitting at Andrew Cavanaugh's table. It was one thing to show up on Callie's doorstep. After three days of being together, he felt as if he'd known her forever, as if he could turn to her during low points in this crisis and somehow, by just knowing she was there, manage to get through it.

But even though he knew Andrew Cavanaugh, it wasn't on the same level. He'd exchanged words with the man on several occasions and they had mutual friends, but that was the extent of it. And as for the others, he wouldn't have known any of them if he'd tripped over them in the street. How rude was it to just drop in on all of them like this?

Very, he decided. His hand covered the key he'd left in the ignition, debating.

Callie got out of her car and looked behind her. Brent had pulled up to the curb at the same time she'd reached the house, but his door wasn't opening.

Had he changed his mind? Or was something else wrong?

She hurried down the driveway. "What's the matter?" she called out.

Brent shook his head. This had been a mistake. "Maybe I shouldn't—"

But he never got a chance to finish what he was about to say. Callie was opening his door. "Maybe you should," she countered, leaving absolutely no room for argument in her voice. Just in case he was having second thoughts, she took hold of his hand and tugged.

Brent had no choice but to get out of the car and follow her into the house.

The front door was unlocked.

This was even worse than her apartment. At least she had her door locked. "Don't you people believe in prevention?"

She closed the door behind him. "Anyone who's going to walk into a houseful of cops to pull off a heist has a death wish and deserves what's coming to him."

Not taking any chances for an abrupt departure, she continued to hold his hand as she led the way to the kitchen.

"There she is, late as usual," Andrew announced to the others at the table. As usual, he didn't bother turning to look at his errant daughter. Instead, taking a plate, he began building a pyramid of pancakes for her.

"The only reason Rayne's here ahead of me is that all she has to do is roll down the stairs," Callie protested. And then, because all five pairs of eyes at the table—she noticed that her cousin Patience had joined them this morning—had turned to look at the

man behind her, she obliged them with an introduc-
tion. "I brought a guest. Everybody, this is Judge
Brenton Montgomery. Brent, this is everybody."

Plate in hand, Andrew turned from the stove to
look in Brent's direction. If he was surprised by the
man's appearance, he hid it well.

Taking charge, Andrew stepped forward. "You do
my table honor, Judge. And you'll excuse my daughter, she has a congenital defect. She was born without
any manners." He handled the introductions properly, going clockwise around the oval table. "This is
Shaw, Teri, Clay and Rayne, my children. And that
perky young woman seated at the far end is my
niece, Patience. My late brother Mike's daughter,"
he added.

"Patience doesn't count," Callie cracked as she
took her place at the table. With a nod of her head,
she indicated the seat next to her. Brent sat down.
"She's a vet."

Patience pretended to take offense at the slight. "I
see all the police personnel I need to when they come
into the office with the K-9 unit."

"So, Judge," Andrew placed the heaping plate of
pancakes he'd compiled in front of Brent instead of
Callie, "what brings you to my table?"

Brent looked at the offering, a little overwhelmed
by the stack. Did people really consume this much
for breakfast? He was accustomed to a piece of toast,
if that much. "Actually, Callie did. I originally
thought we were on the way to the precinct."

Andrew shot an approving look at his daughter.

For her own safety she decided not to make anything of it. "All in good time, Judge," Andrew said. "Can't start a day without a good breakfast."

On Brent's other side, Rayne leaned her head into his and conspiratorially confided, "Can't get away from the table without one, either."

In response, Brent looked at Callie questioningly.

"I guess I should have warned you," Callie murmured. She offered him a smile that he found particularly compelling. You would have thought, he caught himself musing, that he'd been brought to his girlfriend's house to meet her family for the first time. The whole scene smacked of Norman Rockwell.

Were people really that normal out there? he wondered. It actually comforted him in this time of turmoil to believe that they were.

Within moments, despite the emptiness he'd been harboring in his chest since the moment he'd learned of Rachel's abduction, Brent found himself being drawn into this inner circle. The sound of good-natured voices, all trying to top one another, echoed around him.

This was so different from anything he could ever remember at his own table when he'd been growing up. He and his two siblings rarely took breakfast with his parents, and when they had, they were required to be silent. Both his parents subscribed to the ancient adage that children should be seen and not heard.

Obviously, no such edict had ever existed in the

Cavanaugh household. Or, if it did, it was completely ignored.

The din ebbed and swelled. Finally he leaned toward Callie, turning his head so that his mouth was close to her ear. He doubted his voice would carry otherwise. "How can you hear yourself think?"

She grinned, licking a drop of maple syrup from her finger. "I don't have to. Someone else'll tell me what I'm thinking."

Watching her tongue flick along the point of her finger, he felt something tighten within his stomach. He realized he'd stopped talking. And for the moment, stopped breathing, as well.

"More coffee, Judge?"

The voice at his elbow startled him. He did his best not to show it. "All things considered, I think you should call me Brent." In response to Andrew's question, Brent moved his cup to the edge of the table.

Andrew poured and then stood back for a second, looking at Callie and the man she had brought with her. *All things considered, I think I'll be calling you son before long if I don't miss my guess.*

He inclined his head toward Brent. "All right, 'Brent,' I want to see you making short work of that stack of pancakes."

Callie saw the look of dismay on Brent's face and quickly came to his rescue. She nodded at the plate. "Three Egyptians toiling on the pyramids for the Pharaoh couldn't make short work of that, Dad." She shook her head. "You overfeed people."

Andrew eyed his daughter. This one would go to her grave arguing. "Not everyone is content to weigh in at ninety pounds, missy."

The familiar refrain had her packing it in. "Which is my cue to leave." She glanced at her watch. They'd been here longer than she'd intended, but Brent really looked as if he was enjoying himself. He was sorely in need of this distraction and, if nothing else, her family certainly was distracting. She laid a hand on Brent's arm. "We'd better get going." Brent was on his feet immediately.

Andrew frowned, shaking his head in abject disapproval. "Last to arrive, first to go."

Picking up a piece of hardly browned toast, Callie patted her father's cheek. "Always leave them wanting more, isn't that what you taught me?"

"*Them,*" Andrew emphasized, fisted hands on his hips. "Not me."

"Thanks for breakfast," she said over her shoulder, already hurrying to the door.

Brent paused to take his leave properly. He shook hands with Callie's father. "Thanks for having me."

For a moment Andrew gripped the hand that Brent offered, giving it a firm shake. Brent felt as if he'd just entered into a covenant of some kind. "You hang in there," Andrew counseled.

A slight smile on his face, Brent nodded toward the others, grateful that they hadn't all fallen into stupefying silence at his appearance, or that they hadn't awkwardly offered words of comfort. He re-

alized this was just what he needed to give him the
strength to continue.

"Nice family," Brent told Callie as he hurried out
after her.

She turned up the lapels of her jacket. It was
windy this morning. Windy and damp. She wondered
if it was going to rain. "Yeah, I've decided to keep
them. Actually, I don't think I have much of a
choice. They'd overwhelm anyone else." She looked
at him. "Did they overwhelm you?"

"No. They were just what the doctor ordered."
He looked at her before he got into his vehicle. "But
then, you already knew that, didn't you?"

She merely grinned. "I had my suspicions." Her
car purred to life and she backed out of the driveway.

Callie could feel the tension the moment she
walked into the task force room. It took her less than
a heartbeat to discover the source. Seated at her desk
with a police officer posted on either side was Jennifer Montgomery.

The moment she saw them walk into the room,
Jennifer jumped to her feet. Her eyes blazed as she
zeroed in on the woman whose name had been mentioned when she'd been brought in.

"How *dare* you treat me like a suspect!" she
shouted at Callie. Anger smoldered like a smoky
aura. "I was almost dragged from the plane in
chains!"

When confronted with anger, Callie had found that
the best way to combat it was to remain nerve-

numbingly calm. She also consoled herself with the thought that it would probably irritate the hell out of the woman.

"Don't exaggerate, Mrs. Montgomery," Callie said mildly, doing what she felt was a marvelous job of hiding her animosity toward the woman. What kind of mother had to be forcibly brought into the police station when her daughter was missing? She met Jennifer's fiery gaze head-on. "I'm sure no one dragged anyone and there were no chains involved."

Looking angry enough to spit, Jennifer whirled toward Brent. "Are you going to let her talk to me like that?" she demanded.

"Detective Cavanaugh is in charge of this investigation, and if she finds Rachel, she can talk to anyone she wants any way she wants," Brent said.

Her eyes blazed. "Might have known I couldn't depend on you." Enraged, Jennifer turned toward Callie again. "All I know is that you'd better have a damn good reason for having me manhandled or I'm going to sue you and this police department for everything they're worth." Her eyes narrowed as she looked more closely at Callie. "Don't I know you from somewhere?

Callie felt herself stiffening. "I don't travel in your circles, Mrs. Montgomery."

Her lips curved in a sneer. "I already know that, but your face is familiar." And then it seemed to come to her. "Wait, I think…" She looked back and forth between Brent and Callie. "Yes…" There was triumph on her face. "Didn't you pour yourself all over my husband a few years back?"

She'd gone too far. It hadn't taken long. "Jennifer—" Brent warned.

With the smug look of someone restored to the driver's seat, Jennifer patted his arm condescendingly. "Don't worry, dear. All I care about is finding Rachel." Her eyes narrowed again as she looked at Callie. Jennifer flounced down on the seat again. "Now, ask me your questions and let me get the hell out of here." She looked at Brent over Callie's head. "I want you to know I'm hiring a private investigator to find our daughter."

He curbed the urge to ask her if the investigator was perhaps also her latest lover. But there was no point in going there. What she'd done while they were married had been his concern. Now she could have a dozen lovers and it didn't matter to him anymore.

The sooner Callie asked her questions, he told himself, the sooner Jennifer would leave.

Except that she didn't leave.

When the question session was finally over, since she had no car of her own, Jennifer insisted that he drive her home.

"I'll call you a cab," he offered.

"No." Her eyes shifted over to Callie, then back to Brent. "I want you to take me. You owe me that much. Rachel was in your custody when she was kidnapped."

Callie clenched her hands, digging her nails into

her palms. "That isn't fair, Mrs. Montgomery. The judge has no control…"

Jennifer's green eyes washed over her. "I've often said that."

He had to get her out of here before she caused any more of a scene than she already had. Taking hold of Jennifer's arm, he jerked her toward the door. "C'mon, let's go."

Callie watched them leave. He was taking her home. Since the woman resided in Los Angeles, she figured that meant Brent was driving Jennifer to the house they had once shared as man and wife.

A knot tightened around her midsection.

Not her problem, she reminded herself. Her only concern was finding Rachel.

The knot stayed where it was.

Exhausted, Callie let herself into her apartment. Tossing her purse and keys in the general vicinity of the coffee table, she began shedding her clothes as she made her way to the bathroom. Her gun and holster found a home on the sofa instead of its customary place on top of the refrigerator in the kitchen.

A false alarm had sent them hurrying with dread in their hearts to the city dump. To search for Rachel's lifeless body. It had turned out to be a small-boned homeless woman, who, from everything the ME could ascertain, had died of natural causes. As natural as causes for death could be when you were in your late twenties.

Callie silently blessed the foundation her father

had given her, which allowed her to go on after days like today.

All she wanted to do now was to soak in a hot tub until she washed away the grime of the day from her body and then go to bed. Barely digestible hero sandwiches from a lunch truck had made a place for themselves in her stomach where they remained, still making their presence known after eight hours. The thought of food was out of the question right now.

Maybe forever.

She was in the tub before the water had finished filling it. White foam parted as she slipped in. Her eyes closed, she let the heat work its magic and ease the tension from her body.

It took a while.

Despite a mountain of phone tips, they still had no real leads, nothing to grab on to. And by tomorrow morning at eight, four days would have gone by.

"Rest, Callie, rest," she ordered herself. But she felt frustrated no matter what direction she turned in. The case was stymieing her. And then there was the matter of Jennifer's dramatic performance. It hadn't helped any.

Neither had the fact that Brent had taken her home. He'd never returned.

Why should he? she asked herself. He had no real business being at the precinct. Being at her side. Jennifer Montgomery was still a very beautiful woman. And the mother of his child.

Callie wondered if they were together right now. If Jennifer was consoling him at this very moment.

"Not your concern," she announced loudly.

Damn, she should have brought her radio in with her. If it was on loud enough, it could have drowned out her thoughts.

But the only thing she'd brought in with her was the telephone. And it rang now.

Staring at the offensive receiver, Callie sighed. Couldn't whoever it was have waited ten more minutes? And then guilt washed over her. What if this was about Rachel?

With another sigh, Callie braced herself as she reached for the receiver where she'd left it on the floor next to the tub.

"Cavanaugh."

"I just wanted you to know, there's nothing between Jennifer and me anymore." Brent's rich baritone voice filled her ear.

She felt her pulse scrambling as she leaned back in the tub. Dissipating soap suds rallied around her from either side. She could feel her mouth curving. "You don't have to tell me that."

"Yes, yes I do," he insisted firmly. "As little as six months ago, maybe it wouldn't have been true, the answer might have been different, but my feelings for Jennifer have long since been drained away. A little like a bad sinus infection, I guess. I'm over her." There was an awkward pause. "Like I said, I just wanted you to know. I'll see you in the morning."

"Right."

Callie stared at the wireless receiver for a long

while. Waiting for her pulse to become steady, for the unrelated, scattered thoughts to settle down and stop linking up in her head. He hadn't said why he'd stayed away all day, she reminded herself.

Somehow, it didn't matter.

She sank even deeper in the tub, letting the warmth take her away. And smiled.

Chapter 11

Brent felt the dirt crumbling beneath his right foot and stepped back from the edge of the ravine just as a small shower of gravel and earth rained down below.

A little more than ten feet beneath him, a team comprised of police and firefighters were working to retrieve the lifeless body of a child and raise it up to level ground.

He held his breath for an indeterminable length of time. Praying for the best, he expected the worst, despite all his efforts to block those thoughts from his mind.

As the light faded the din around him continued. The rescuers were working swiftly, although there was no life to save any longer.

Was it Rachel?

Oh, God, he hoped not.

He was barely aware of Callie being by his side. She'd kept him apprised of everything that was or wasn't happening. It was day number four, and until an hour ago there had been no progress despite the best efforts of the Aurora police force.

He prayed there was no progress now. That that small body discovered by some hikers wasn't his Rachel. He wasn't sure if he could hold it together if it was.

An Amber Alert was out, flashing across the bottom of television screens, blinking bright yellow lights to commuters on all the freeways, inviting the public to come forth with any information, however minute it might seem, in order to help them solve this heinous crime.

All the bus drivers who had driven past Bristol and Oak in either direction any time within an hour of the estimated time of abduction had been called in for questioning by the police to see if they had noticed anything. No one had.

Numbly, Brent looked at a piece of paper that flapped noisily in the late-fall breeze against the utility pole. It was a flyer with Rachel's picture and description, identical to thousands of other flyers that his friends and volunteers had placed on every available surface in and around Aurora, hoping to jar someone's memory. Hoping to get a clue that would bring his baby back to him.

Staring straight down, watching the rescuers, Brent shoved his clenched hands deep inside the pockets of his navy windbreaker. He wasn't accustomed to this kind of inertia. He was a doer, a man who had never allowed himself to stand on the sidelines. Yet here he was, on the sidelines, completely impotent, completely at a loss as to what to do.

He'd already gone on the air, not once, but twice, to offer a substantial reward for any word that would help lead to Rachel's recovery. The only thing the second appearance had led to was an upsurge in phone calls to the police station. There was now an entire separate unit set up to handle the calls, trying to winnow out the genuine ones from the crazies.

Several of the calls that had come in reported seeing a girl fitting Rachel's description sitting in the rear passenger seat of a black or navy-blue Mercedes 500SL. One caller had the car heading north, the other three had the car going south.

Brent felt like a dog chasing his own tail, running in circles and going nowhere.

This morning there were three bands of local Scout troops out, moving in slow motion at arm's length, searching the surrounding parks in the area. Looking for clues.

Looking for Rachel's body.

Brent stifled the shiver that went over his own. There was no getting away from that reality. She could be dead. He'd presided over enough cases to know that reality could be grim.

It shouldn't be, he thought, not for a five-year-old. For a five-year-old, life should be nothing but ice cream, merry-go-rounds and laughter and Christmas morning.

Please God, let me have Christmas morning with her, he prayed.

But Christmas morning was still weeks away. And he was standing here now, at the edge of the wilderness preserve, fear throbbing in his heart. Awaiting word that might very well forever destroy any Christmas morning he could ever hope to experience.

Twilight descended on the area. It would be dark soon. The men worked as quickly as they could. The call had just come in less than an hour ago. Hikers had found a body. He'd been with Callie in her office at the time.

His heart had shouted ''No!'' even as his mind whispered the worst word in the world: Maybe.

The rescuers were almost done. Callie looked at Brent. By all rights she should have gone down with the others to help recover the small corpse, but she'd sent Ramon Diaz in her place. Someone had to remain here with Brent.

The man looked as if he were a granite stature, about to be shattered by one well-placed, strategic blow. She prayed that he wouldn't receive it. ''You shouldn't be here.''

His eyes shifted toward her. ''Where should I be?'' he demanded heatedly. All the frustration he felt came pouring out at once. He was powerless to stop it. ''At home, throwing back a brandy? My little girl's out there somewhere, going through God knows what, waiting for me to come and rescue her.

Maybe even down there—'' He stopped, unable to finish.

The gurney the recovery team was hoisting out of the area appeared over the edge of the ravine. The small body was only a few feet away now.

Brent caught his breath. Afraid.

Callie turned and placed herself between Brent and the stretcher. She wanted to see it first before he did. To prepare him if she had to.

The small body was badly decomposed. Too decomposed to be his daughter. She let out a long sigh of relief. ''It's not Rachel.'' Turning to Brent, she explained, ''Whoever this is has been here longer than four days. It's not Rachel,'' she repeated.

Grateful, he nodded, backing off. Backing away. His eyes stung badly.

Callie was torn for a moment as to just where her duty lay. Making a decision, she looked at Diaz. ''Get the body to the M.E. I want identification as soon as possible.'' Her heart aching, she looked down at the remains of what had once been a human being. *Who did this to you, little one?* There were times she truly hated her job. ''This is somebody's child.''

''Right away, Cal,'' Diaz replied. He looked at the team of rescuers. ''You heard the lady, we're going to the M.E.''

Brent was standing off to the side. Callie went to him. His back to her, she gently laid a hand on his shoulder.

''Let me get you home.'' His back remained rigid.

"This wasn't Rachel," she told him for the third time.

"No, it wasn't. Thank God." There was a look of anger in his eyes as he turned around to face her. He scrubbed his hands over his face, hating the ambivalent feelings that were bouncing around inside of him. "Here I am, rejoicing because that body isn't my daughter. Rejoicing because someone else has to hear those words and not me." He'd always thought of himself as being compassionate. Now he didn't know. "What kind of person does that make me?"

"A parent," she answered quietly. It tore her up to see him this way. Too close, she was getting too close to all of this. She knew it was no way to operate, that being close, making it personal, took away her edge. But she couldn't help herself. Any more than she could take herself off the case. "Focus on the positive, Brent. That's the only way any of us ever gets through a day. Focus on the positive," she repeated. She took hold of his arm. "Let's go."

After a moment he inclined his head and allowed himself to be ushered away from the scene.

There was paperwork waiting for her, but she let it wait. Right now she had something more pressing to take care of.

Callie drove straight to Brent's house and pulled her Crown Victoria into his driveway. They'd hardly talked at all on the way over. She'd tried to beat back the silence several times, but the conversation had remained one-sided, with Brent hardly offering a word in response.

Couldn't say she hadn't tried, Callie thought.

Only the front lights were on. They cast a bleak, haunting illumination along the front walk. His sister and brother-in-law, she knew, had gone back to their own lives. Still concerned about their niece, they needed to see to their own family.

At least there would be no one asking him questions tonight, she thought. Brent needed peace and quiet.

Her foot on the brake, she looked at him. "I'll see you tomorrow."

Brent put his hand on the door handle, then stopped as he looked at the empty house. "Callie?"

"Yes?"

He turned to look at her. "Come in with me. I don't want to be alone tonight."

Her eyes met his. Something stirred within her. The same something that she'd felt the first time Brent had approached her at the fund-raiser and asked her to dance. Except more so.

She knew what would happen if she agreed to come in with him.

If she stayed.

Feelings that had gone dormant the instant Kyle had been killed suddenly sprang back into existence. They pressed forward. But even as they did, she remembered all the pain, all the heartache that was attached to feeling something for someone, that came with loving someone.

Brent wasn't asking her for love, he was asking her to keep the shadows at bay.

Didn't matter what he was asking, Callie thought, she still knew what would happen. How she would respond. She wasn't a woman who believed in casual liaisons. Her heart had always been in everything she did. And her heart, she reminded herself, had been badly wounded once.

The light within the vehicle was poor, but she could still see the pain in Brent's eyes as he looked at her. The pain and the need.

It wasn't in her to say no.

"Then you won't be," she replied quietly.

With that she got out of the car.

Brent followed her in silence. She moved aside at the entrance. Brent took out his key and opened the front door.

"You told me not to give up hope," he said without looking at her. "That they would find Rachel."

"Yes?" This was going somewhere, Callie thought, hoping the final destination was at a place she could handle.

"What do you think the odds are?" he asked her, trying to sound detached. Trying to sound as if his whole world wasn't riding on her answer.

She softly closed the door behind her. The sound still echoed in her brain. "Miracles don't have odds, they just happen."

There was a challenge in his eyes as he turned them on her. "So you're telling me that it's going to take a miracle to find her?"

He was twisting things. She reminded herself that he'd been a lawyer, one of the best, if she was to believe her father. That meant he knew his way around words, how to make them bend to his will.

The more tense his tone, the calmer she became. She supposed it had something to do with the yin and yang of a situation.

"I'm telling you that every child we find alive is a miracle, that every hostage situation that's resolved satisfactorily is a miracle. That every breath we take is a miracle. There's an X factor involved in everything, something that defies calculation. It throws off equations," she said, "but it makes things happen."

The expression on his face was completely unreadable. "Is that what they're teaching you now at the police academy?"

She shook her head. "No, that's something I picked up at my father's knee." Callie nodded toward the kitchen. "Now, why don't you let me get you some dinner?"

The thought of food turned his stomach. "I don't want any dinner."

He could at least go through the motions, swallowing a few forkfuls. She debated what to make. "You have to eat, Brent. You can't keep running on empty."

He looked at her. She'd been at his side throughout the whole ordeal. Granted, it was her job, but comforting him wasn't. And she had known just what to say. And when not to say anything at all. He was grateful.

And very drawn to her.

Whether it was because of the situation and the moment was something he didn't feel like exploring. He was only aware of the end result. And that he wanted her.

''I don't need food right now.''

She knew exactly what he needed. What they both, in their own ways, needed. And she surrendered herself to it. To him. To the burning need to fill the emptiness within her own soul.

Callie held her breath, willing her heart to cease hammering as Brent slowly swept his long fingers over her cheek, tilting her head up just slightly with his thumb.

And then his lips were on hers and any orders she'd left with the rest of her body disintegrated without a trace.

It was as if she'd been waiting for this all along. Since before there was a way to gauge time.

A contented sigh racking her body, her arms went around his neck. She cleaved her body to his as the kiss erupted from something soft to something questing and erotic.

Gentleness gave way to urgency, to need.

The breath she'd been holding evaporated as heat consumed her, licking at her body from all sides.

She wanted this, needed this. Desired this. Desired him.

With sure, capable hands, she began unbuttoning his shirt, her mouth never leaving his. Savoring the tangy sweetness of his lips.

She wanted nothing else but to be his. If comfort came later, his, hers, theirs, so be it. But right now there was an overpowering need just to be possessed.

She felt she couldn't see another sunrise without it happening. Without his taking her the way a man took a woman he cared about.

And if in the morning she discovered that she'd fabricated things in her own mind to justify what she was doing right now, so be it.

All that mattered was now.

He wasn't thinking clearly, he knew that, but it wasn't the time to think. Thinking hurt. Feeling hurt, and yet he was feeling.

Feeling what? Lust? Desire? He wasn't sure. All Brent knew was that the pain humming now through his body was a good pain. It was a feeling of coming home, of finding a way to renew himself in something that was life affirming.

Callie was everything he had once hoped he would find in a woman who would swear to spend the rest of her life by his side. What he'd once hoped, blindly, he had found in Jennifer.

But in Jennifer, there had been only emptiness; the words that had been sworn to had covered shallowness. The irony of it would have amused him had his senses not been spinning faster than the speed of light right now.

Holding Callie, kissing her, desiring her, was causing an electrical storm to erupt within him. Every kiss demanded another, every touch fed on itself, begging for more. Always more.

He began to wonder if he would ever be satiated.

Brent could feel her fingers flying along his skin as she unbuttoned his shirt. He tugged her jacket off her arms, letting it fall to the floor, then realized that there was a bigger obstacle between them than her blouse and bra.

He drew back as his fingers came in contact with leather.

Immediately aware of the problem, Callie drew back, her insides shaking.

"Give me a sec," she murmured, unhooking the holster that kept her service revolver in place.

The safety was on, but she knew better than to underestimate the power of her weapon. She lowered it to the floor on top of her jacket.

"Better?" she murmured against his mouth.

"Better." The word tasted of sin and desire and everything that had been missing from her life for so long.

And then there was no time for words, no need for words.

She shivered in anticipation as she felt his fingers parting her blouse. The feel of his hands along her skin caused everything to tighten inside. She felt like a coil ready to spring with the least possible encouragement.

It was not long in coming.

A moment later her blouse was gone, along with her bra, and she was pressed against his bare skin. Feeling it. Feeling the heat that ignited from the mere contact of skin to skin.

She wondered if her heart would eventually hammer its way out of her chest. It would be worth it because she felt as if she'd been caught up in some wild, raging river. She was being swept out to sea and she didn't care.

Brent dove his fingers into her hair, framing her face before he brought his mouth down to hers again. He was holding her, kissing her, until she was reduced to a pulsating puddle.

And then she felt his hands leaving her face, traveling down the length of her until they came to the single button that held her pleated, pinstripe trousers in place. Callie caught her breath, her abdomen all but froze as she felt him release it.

The next moment he was placing his hands on either side of her hips. Coaxing the fabric from her body. Every nerve ending stood at attention as he deliberately made slow progress, freeing her flesh, readying it for his touch.

Her pulse throbbing in her throat, at her wrists, in her loins, Callie hurried to mimic his movements. She felt as if she was using someone else's hands. She was numb and pulsating all at the same time.

And breathing was a definite challenge now. Her breath came in short, shallow snatches as her pulse raced and her heart threatened to take off.

With a squeal of triumph, she kicked aside her own clothing and then drew aside his.

Their bodies branded each other.

Over and over again, his mouth sought hers, his hands caressing her even as his kisses grew more intense, more demanding. She felt as if her knees were dissolving. All the strength she possessed was being drained from her body at lightning speed.

And then she felt herself being laid upon the wide, dark sofa. She could feel the marshmallow leather swallowing her up at the same time that Brent was drawing her toward him.

She was surprised the sofa didn't catch fire. Her body had to be beyond the incinerating point.

Callie threaded her legs around his torso. She was ready for him.

Looming over Callie, his hands braced on either side of her head, Brent looked at her. He was more than half-dazed, his brain foggy about how they had come so far so quickly. This wasn't his way. He was afraid that he'd pushed an advantage he shouldn't have.

He wanted her with a fierceness that under any other circumstances would have scared the hell out of him, but he needed to know that she wanted this, too.

Otherwise, he needed to back away. As if he could.

She felt air rushing in, air where his lips had been a moment ago. She opened her eyes and saw him looking at her.

"Callie—"

Oh, no. No talking, not now, not when every part of her body was quivering. Waiting. Wanting.

"Callie," he began again. "If I rushed you…" If? his brain mocked. He'd stripped her down to her eyelashes and they hadn't been in his house for more than fifteen minutes. "You don't have to do this if you don't want to."

He couldn't have said anything better. She could see he struggled to control himself. Struggled to hold back, almost as much as she was.

"You sure know how to pick your moments, Judge," she whispered against his mouth, her breath teasing him. "Permission to approach the bench, Your Honor."

"Permission granted."

She arched her hips. Giving in to his need, he sealed his mouth to hers as he drove into her.

Finally finding solace.

Chapter 12

Brent didn't realize that he'd fallen asleep until he opened his eyes. Automatically he looked to his right. The place beside him on the wide four-poster was empty.

Callie was gone.

He sat up immediately. Had there been a call about Rachel? Or had her abrupt departure been triggered by another reason.

They'd gone fast; faster than anything he would have anticipated or prophesied. But what had happened here tonight hadn't been about planning. Looking back, he knew that it had been about the inevitable.

Their coming together had been just a matter of time. And nothing had ever felt so right. They'd made love twice before coming up to the bedroom where they'd made love one more time and fallen asleep in each other's arms.

But something had obviously gone wrong after that. Had she been plagued by second thoughts? Regrets?

Throwing back the covers, Brent swung his legs off the bed. His trousers were on the floor, and he quickly pulled them on, intending to go looking for her.

Two steps across the floor and he halted.

Callie was sitting on the window seat, staring out into the darkness. Her legs tucked in under her, her long blond hair tousled about her shoulders, she was wearing his shirt to cover her nakedness.

He'd never seen anything so sexy in his life.

Brent watched her for a long moment in silence before saying anything. He felt as if he was breaking some kind of spell.

"I thought you'd left."

She'd thought about it. But where would she go? Everywhere she went, she would have had to take herself along, and she was the problem. Or, more specifically, what was in her mind.

Memories.

Guilt mingled with fear in a macabre dance that refused to end.

She continued to look out the window, searching for a way to regain control over her thoughts, over her feelings. Both eluded her.

"No," she replied softly, "I'm right here."

Brent came up behind her, looking at her reflection

in the window. She looked sad. Was he responsible for that? "Are you all right?"

She could feel tears rising and upbraided herself for being so weak, so vulnerable. "Yes."

He knew he should back off, but he couldn't let it go. "You don't sound all right."

That was because she wasn't, Callie thought. Not really. She tightened her arms around herself, as if that could somehow keep the sadness at bay. Make the fear disappear.

The confession came of its own volition. "I haven't been with a man since Kyle…" She left it at that. Try as she might, she couldn't force herself to utter the word *died.*

Callie felt his hands on her shoulders and raised her eyes to look at his reflection in the window. The glass diminished the kindness, but she could still see it in his eyes.

"That makes two of us," he told her quietly.

A teasing grin came out of nowhere, spawned in self-defense against the sadness. She covered one hand with her own, taking solace in the unspoken comfort that was offered.

"You haven't been with a man since Kyle, either?"

He laughed, grateful for the break in tension. "No, but I haven't been with a woman since my marriage broke up."

She did a quick calculation. If she remembered correctly, his marriage had broken up over four years ago. Letting his hand go, she turned around to look at him. "Not once?"

"Not once." It wasn't the kind of thing a man freely admitted, especially a man who was as private as he was, but somehow, telling her seemed all right. "I kind of lost faith in my capability to make good personal judgments." The irony of the situation brought a sad smile to his lips. "I feel pretty secure in my abilities to make good calls on the bench, but as far as my private life goes, well," he shrugged, "you met Jennifer. I'd say my abilities in that area turned out to be pretty much of a bust."

"One wrong judgment doesn't brand you for life. Give yourself a break," she urged. "Everyone's entitled to make a mistake." Her mouth curved. Mercifully the sadness was beginning to slip away. "And, speaking off the record, I'd say that not all your calls in that area were bad."

The light within her eyes warmed something within him. Brent wove his fingers through her hair, framing her head with his hands.

He could feel his smile beginning in his eyes and blossoming until it had reached his lips, taking his complete countenance with it.

"No, I guess they're not."

He sat down next to her, gathering her to him. Callie resisted a moment, her independent streak getting the better of her. And then she allowed herself to lean on Brent. A very faint scent of cologne still clung to him and she breathed it in, letting it settle her nerves.

Brent stroked her hair. "Do you want to tell me about Kyle?"

They would have liked each other, she thought. Both were men of integrity, men you could count on. Her heart ached a little.

"He was a great cop. A great guy. And he died all too young. I loved him a great deal. At first I didn't want to." She bit her lip, remembering. After a moment she continued, "I was afraid. But he just kept after me and finally wore me down. I loved him with all my heart. I don't hold back when I feel something."

Brent kissed her forehead, holding her close. "Yes, I know." He didn't know this because someone had told him, it was just something he felt. Just as he felt that if anyone could help him find Rachel, it was Callie.

He kissed her forehead again. And then each of her eyelids as they fluttered shut.

Callie turned her mouth up to his.

Desire stirred again, seizing him tightly as if it hadn't already visited him three times tonight and been spent. He was thirty-eight years old, and she made him feel as if he was a college freshman, involved in his very first serious love affair.

He wanted her again, wanted her so badly he could barely breathe.

Still kissing her, Brent rose, picking her up in his arms. He walked back to his bed, wanting only to make love with her again. To lose himself in the softness, in the passion that was Callie.

Gently he placed her on the rumpled bed and joined her. The shirt she'd slipped on wasn't buttoned, and it parted about her body. He could feel a quickening in his loins, could feel the ache for her growing.

But instead of giving in to the increasing demands of his body, he paused to caress her face, to look at the woman who had given herself to him at a price higher than he'd realized.

"I won't hurt you, Callie," he whispered.

Her heart ached so badly, she thought it would break right then and there. She placed her hand over his. "Don't make promises you can't keep."

He smiled at her, recalling what she'd said to him earlier when they'd begun this awful search for his daughter. "All we have is our faith and our hope to see us through."

"Ouch." She laughed softly, shaking her head. He'd left his trousers unbuttoned, and they'd slipped from his waist as he'd lain down. Callie cradled the palm of her hand along his hip line, feeling the seeds of desire taking root. "You would have perfect recall."

"It's a small enough trade-off." His eyes washed over her, heating her blood. "You have perfect everything else."

"I had no idea you had such a gift of gab." Her eyes teased him, belying the excitement that had begun raging within her. Callie positioned herself so that she was almost beneath him, then pulled him closer. "Now shut up and kiss me, Judge."

His body covered hers. "With pleasure, Detective."

And then she was lost, lost in the flames that surrounded her, cutting off any hope for a successful exit. Not that she wanted any. What she wanted was for tomorrow not to come, for this to go on forever.

She kissed him hard, putting her very soul into it. The soul that she'd suddenly found again.

But she couldn't delude herself, pretend that this was going to last forever. *Forever* was a word that poets used. It didn't apply to mortals, and she felt very, very mortal at this moment.

But if she couldn't have forever, or even tomorrow, at least she could have now, and now was all she would ask for. All she wanted. To have him continue to blot out everything else, the world, its overwhelming weight and responsibilities. Everything. Leaving only the two of them on this giant bed that had never known love before tonight if she was to believe him.

And she did. With all of her healing heart.

In the blink of an eye, Callie turned into a tigress in his arms, sparking new emotions from within him, causing him to go to new depths, new heights all at the same time. Digging responses out of him that he hadn't known existed. Ever.

Their bodies heated, their limbs entwined. Brent kissed and was kissed over and over again until he felt as if he'd become some throbbing, mindless mass of flesh that had been created solely for this purpose, for this moment. And, most important, for this woman.

His heart, kept in isolation all these years, accessible only to his daughter, broke out of its self-imposed prison and beat. Hard.

For Callie.

Brent kissed every inch of her, learning the shape and contour of her body by sight, by touch, by taste until it was completely, indelibly imprinted on his mind, never to be erased. Not by time, not by circumstances, perhaps not even by death.

In that final moment, before he slipped into her, taking what was already his, Brent committed himself to her.

Completely.

Silently.

Sheathed in her body, he held himself in check, going slowly but then at an ever-increasing tempo until restraint was impossible.

Her hard breathing echoing in his head, he unleashed the reins he'd kept around his passion and allowed himself to enjoy the final rush. Enjoying her cry of ecstasy even more.

She'd cried out his name and it resounded over and over again in his head. Brent tightened his arms around her, holding her and the moment to him as closely as he could.

Wanting it to last. Knowing it couldn't.

But knowing the memory would.

''I think the earth moved just then,'' he heard her

murmur against his chest. Her breath warmed him. Almost as much as holding her did.

If there had been an earthquake, he would have been too wrapped up around her to have known about it. Especially since he'd been experiencing one of his own, right in this bed.

He sighed, a true contentment undulating slowly along his body. He secretly blessed her for this respite. "We can check the news later."

"I'm not sure the Richter scale can accommodate this kind of quake." She raised her head to look at him. Playfully crossing her arms on his chest, Callie rested her head against them. Her eyes sparkled as she regarded him. "So that's what you've been hiding beneath those judicial robes of yours."

He smiled at her because she made him feel like smiling all over. Something that he hadn't felt like doing in a very long time.

"I'm afraid that's going to have to remain a secret, Detective."

She pretended to seal her lips. "They won't get it out of me."

Something was going on inside of her. Something she didn't want to identify or give a name to just yet. Something serious. But she didn't want anything to spoil the moment or detract from it.

She was about to bring her mouth down to his when the strains of the "William Tell Overture" broke the silence and nudged aside the sensual mood that was once more building up between them.

Her eyes widened as a different kind of adrenaline kicked in.

Rolling over to her right, Callie reached for her phone, only to find that she hadn't left it on the nightstand as was her custom at home.

"Damn," she muttered.

Callie was on her feet instantly, moving aside discarded bits of clothing in her search for the lost cell phone. Brent joined her, but it was Callie, on her hands and knees, who finally discovered the phone on its third go-round of what had become known as the "Lone Ranger's" theme song. Somehow the cell had gotten kicked under the bed.

Opening it, she brought the cell to her ear as she dragged her free hand through her hair, trying to do the same to her brain.

"Cavanaugh," she cried breathlessly, hoping the other party hadn't hung up.

"Callie? It's three in the morning, why do you sound as if you've just run a marathon?"

Adams. Was this his idea of a joke? Or was he checking up on her just to be perverse? "Because I have," she snapped, as no plausible excuse came to her. The last thing she wanted was to have Adams start guessing why she sounded so breathless. "Now why don't you tell me why you're calling me at three in the morning?"

"We found the car."

Every nerve ending in her body went on the alert as Callie pressed the small instrument against her ear,

praying the signal wouldn't cut out until she got the
pertinent information.

''Where?''

Adams paused for a moment. It was evident from
his voice that he was feeling pretty smug. Never
mind that it had probably been one of the patrolmen
who had discovered the car, Callie thought.

''North, heading out of Aurora. It was abandoned
behind one of those signs they used to say highway
patrol officers hid behind, waiting to make a speeding collar.''

She could feel her excitement heightening. Callie
thought back to the four calls they'd received that
had placed Rachel in a Mercedes, heading out of the
city. Only one had said north.

This could finally be the first real break they'd
gotten.

''Are you sure it's the one?''

''A 2002 Navy Mercedes 500 SL,'' Adams recited. ''The CSI team is going over it right now, but
it looks pretty hopeful.''

Her eyes met Brent's. She could see the anticipation, the anxiety. Callie nodded her head. ''Who does
it belong to?''

''I've got Diaz on that right now. There's no reg-
istration in the glove compartment,'' Adams told her.
''Car's been picked clean.''

''Stripped?'' Though the CSI team was more than
capable, she needed to see the vehicle for herself to
satisfy the questions in her mind.

''No, I mean whoever drove the car left nothing

inside. It's showroom pristine. All that's missing is the new car smell.''

"They *always* overlook something,'' she insisted. "No matter how small.'' Callie gathered her clothes together as she talked to her former partner. "Give me your exact location.''

He sounded annoyed at the intrusion he obviously knew was coming. "We've got it covered, Cavanaugh. Why don't you go back to your marathon?''

His tone was exactly why they weren't partners anymore. The detective had called to thump his chest. He hadn't foreseen that she was going to insist on being there. But as primary, she reserved the right to be on the scene any time a clue was uncovered.

Her own tone was firm. "I don't feel like arguing with you, Adams.'' She heard the man on the other end sigh, and then, like a prisoner being tortured, he told her the freeway exit she needed to use. "Great, I can be there in half an hour.''

"I'll throw an extra shrimp on the bar-be,'' he deadpanned, doing little to disguise his annoyance.

"Don't go to any trouble.''

With that, Callie slapped the cell phone closed and scrambled up to her feet.

Brent was on her immediately.

"What?'' he wanted to know. He'd barely been able to hold back the questions, the fearful anticipation, as he'd listened to the one-sided conversation. "Is it Rachel? Did they find her.''

"Not her, but Adams thinks they've found the car used in the kidnapping. An abandoned 2002 navy

Mercedes 500 SL. It's just off of I5.'' Impatient to get going, she pressed her clothes against her. There wasn't time for a shower. She needed to get there now. "Forensics is going over it right now."

He crossed to his closet, taking out a fresh shirt. "I'm coming with you."

She opened her mouth to tell him that there wasn't anything he could do, that what was happening beyond the city outskirts was going to be painstakingly slow. But he didn't need to hear that. To banish him from the scene was tantamount to cruel and unusual punishment. She couldn't bring herself to do it.

She stripped off his shirt and began to get dressed in her own clothes.

"We need to hurry," she told him. "Adams has a tendency to take over investigations, and I want to look at that abandoned Mercedes myself."

Brent was dressed before she finished her sentence.

Chapter 13

Framed against the darkness and illuminated by the billboard lights, the car didn't look like the kind that would be abandoned so carelessly.

Callie circled the Mercedes slowly, as if waiting for the vehicle to talk to her. The odometer had less than five thousand miles on it. This had been someone's pride and joy. Not the kind of vehicle to be used in the commission of a crime.

Stolen? Callie chewed on her bottom lip as she completed her circumnavigation. If it was stolen, then why hadn't there been a report of a missing Mercedes matching this description filed in the past few weeks? She'd gone over the records. There was nothing.

"You know what I said about there not being a

mark on the car?'' Adams said just as she came to the end of her cursory perusal.

Callie raised her eyes over the hood of the car, looking at him. ''Yes?''

There was a lengthy pause, as if the words tasted unusually bitter in his mouth, before he finally· said, ''Well, you were right.''

Her eyes narrowed. She knew it cost her ex-partner to admit that, knew too that he wasn't the type who withheld things just to make himself look good. He was a decent cop; they just didn't get along. But there was a lot of that going around. All she wanted right now was a decent cop, not a soul mate.

Beside her, she could all but feel the tension in Brent's body as he hung on every word, every new finding. This was hell for him, she thought. But there was no way to make this go any faster than it was going.

''What kind of mark?'' she wanted to know. Taking a step back, she knew the answer before he gave it. ''On the grille?''

Adams nodded. ''You got it. Blood. Washed off, but...'' He let his voice trail off as one of the CSI team passed a wandlike device over the area in question. It had been sprayed with luminol, a substance that showed blood in the dark even after it had seemingly been washed off. Since it was still dark, the opportunity to make use of the chemical seemed perfect. The light blue illumination from the wand highlighted small splatters that appeared darker than the rest of the grille. Splatters that weren't evident to the naked eye. Blood splatters.

It took little for Callie to visualize the impact that had caused the telltale signs. She looked at the CSI agent as he shut off the device. "Anything we can match to the nanny's DNA?"

The investigator, a man with more than twenty years on the job, who prided himself on his thoroughness, nodded. "Enough."

She glanced toward Brent, feeling heartened. They were getting somewhere. "Terrific." She looked around toward the people working the scene. "Where's Diaz?"

"Right here." The short, squat man came up from behind her. He flipped open his misshapen notepad. "The car's registered to a Benjamin Jackson."

The name nudged something in Brent's brain, teasing him for a moment before he remembered. He moved out of the background, placing his hand on the older detective's shoulder. The other man turned around to look at him.

"Did you say Ben Jackson?"

Diaz's eyes slid toward Callie before they returned to Brent. His tone was guarded. "Yes."

Callie looked at Brent. Had they found the connection? "You know him?"

"I'm not sure." It wasn't that uncommon a name. He needed more. "Do you know if he was once a vice president at Saunders Computers?"

Diaz frowned, shaking his head. He flipped his notepad closed. "No, but I can find out."

"Why?" Callie asked as Diaz hurried off to his car. She tried to remember seeing the name in the Saunders file, but couldn't. She'd done a great deal of reading that night. "Is that important?"

"Maybe." Brent didn't know, but at least there appeared to be some kind of a tie-in. It was more than they'd had before. "Jackson gave testimony in my court in exchange for immunity."

She didn't see the reason for Jackson to want any kind of revenge against Brent. Had Saunders reached out from prison? Blackmailed Jackson into doing this? "Then you never sent him away."

"No. I sent his boss away." His eyes met Callie's. "On his testimony."

"You must have tried hundreds of cases," Adams interrupted impatiently. "Why would you remember that particular one? What's so special about it?"

The detective was right, Brent thought. He wouldn't have, ordinarily. "It was my first case as a trial judge." His mouth curved in a smile devoid of humor. "You remember those kinds of details before the others come along to blur things."

Maybe it made sense, maybe it didn't. But at least they had something to go on. Callie turned to the detective. "Okay, Adams, take a couple of uniforms and pay Mr. Jackson a visit. Find out what his Mercedes has been up to recently, and if he says it's been stolen, I'd like to hear why he didn't report it missing."

Brent looked into the vehicle. The keys were still in the ignition, an open invitation to anyone who passed by and saw the car. He felt Callie looking at him and glanced at her over his shoulder. "It looks as if whoever drove this car last was hoping someone would come along and steal it."

"The best-laid plans of mice and men..." she murmured with a shake of her head. She nodded at Adams. "Call me as soon as you find out anything."

The noise behind her drew her attention. A flatbed tow truck had arrived to take the Mercedes back to the CSI lab for further analysis.

Stepping back out of the way, she turned toward Brent. He looked tired. Like a man who had been taken for a roller-coaster ride one too many times. A protectiveness stirred within her. The tenderness that came in its wake surprised her. She knew she was getting too involved. She wanted to send him home to sleep until this was all resolved. No one should have to go through what he was experiencing.

"Just how much bad blood is there between you and this Saunders?" She'd asked the question before, but maybe this experience had jarred something loose in his mind. They needed every shred they could find.

Brent had been trying to relive the case in his mind ever since Diaz had mentioned the name. "All I can remember is that when they took him out of the courtroom, he kept shouting, 'You took away my life, you took away my life.'"

She shook her head. "Everyone is always looking for someone else to blame. Ramon," she called to the older detective, who was just getting out of his car again. The man came to her. "I want you to go over to Pelican Bay State Prison and pay Mr. Saunders a visit." She knew Adams hadn't gotten to the man yet. He was still working his way down the list she'd compiled. "See if you can pick up anything from the conversation that might shed a little more light on all this."

The dark head nodded. "Oh, and by the way," he looked at Brent, "I just checked with records. Jackson *was* the VP at Saunders Computers."

Closer, Brent thought. They were getting closer. But were they going to be in time?

They were just getting out of Callie's car as the tow truck pulled into the federal parking lot. There had been little more than silence accompanying them on the ride back. Brent was lost in thought, wondering if he could have done something to prevent the tragedy that had occurred.

Callie got out, looking at him. "Stop blaming yourself. This isn't your fault."

He looked at her sharply, wondering if his expression had given him away. "You've added mind reading to your list of accomplishments?"

"I can sense things about certain people."

"Certain people?"

She shrugged, looking away. The truck rumbled past them. "People I'm close to—usually." She tacked on the last word as if it could somehow protect her from what she'd just said.

"Callie—"

He was going to say something about her not misunderstanding, she thought. That what had taken place between them was something that happened between two consenting adults in times of stress. That she shouldn't make anything of it.

She was ahead of him, ready to blot out any impression she might have accidentally given him. But her cell phone rang just then, curtailing any exchange. Callie sighed. "I've got to get an unlisted number," she quipped, secretly grateful for the rescue out of the awkward moment. "Cavanaugh."

It was Adams. His tone didn't sound encouraging. "Callie, I think you'd better get down here. This case has just hit another bump in the road."

The last time Adams had called her by her first name, he'd attempted to offer words of condolence over Kyle's death. Trying not to look in Brent's direction, she braced herself for the worst.

"What kind of a bump?"

"The kind made by a six-foot, three-inch body."

She closed her eyes. Another dead end? Damn it, they were supposed to be getting closer, not grinding to a halt. "Whose?"

"Jackson's." Adams rattled off the information. "We found him in his study. Someone put a bullet in the back of his head, execution-style. Looks pretty cold-blooded to me. From the smell, I don't think he was the man behind the wheel when the judge's daughter was taken. This man's getting ripe."

So near and yet so far. "Terrific. I'll be right there."

"It's not like he's going anywhere," Adams commented before ringing off.

She saw the look in Brent's eyes. He was on tenterhooks. She was quick to fill him in. "Our best bet just turned up dead."

Brent's mind jumped ahead. She'd sent one of her people to the state prison. "Saunders?"

She shook her head. "Jackson. That was Adams. He just found Jackson shot dead in his study. Execution-style."

She was getting into her car instead of going into the lab. He opened the passenger side door, refusing to be left behind. "Where are we going?"

She was about to tell him to stay behind, but the look in his eyes stopped her. He had a right to be there, she thought. If not legally, then emotionally. "To Jackson's house to see if the killer left any calling cards we can use to link him to your daughter's kidnapping."

Callie started up the car. She knew that the two incidents could be completely unrelated, one of those freaky coincidences that life enjoyed throwing at the police. But she had a gut feeling there was a connection.

Callie glanced at Brent as they pulled out of the parking lot again. "Why don't you give me as many details as you can remember about this first case of yours?"

Since they'd gone over the cases so recently, it took no effort on his part to recall it. "Saunders was a near genius who fancied himself the next Bill

Gates. He got a few backers together and started up his own computer company. It's an old story. Things went very well for a few years and his stock kept going up. He began to live beyond his means until it got completely out of hand. In the interim, you know what happened to the stock market. His stock was no different. It began to drop, the company ran into trouble.'' This they had gotten based on Jackson's information. ''In an attempt to weather the storm, Saunders did a little creative bookkeeping, hoping to stay afloat until things turned around again.''

Callie shook her head. Brent was right. It was an old story, one most would have learned from by now. She got on the freeway, heading south. ''In the meantime, he was defrauding the stockholders,'' she said.

''In a nutshell. Declaring profits when there weren't any, trying to drive the price of stock back up again so that he could cash in himself.'' The plan had been to sell high, then buy back low. The profit would have allowed him to replace stolen money and keep the company afloat. Except it hadn't turned out that way. Jackson turned on his best friend. ''The Security Exchange Commission got wind of it, cornered Jackson to testify against Saunders in exchange for a get-out-of-jail-free card.''

At the time, he had been struck by Saunders's refusal to see the writing on the wall, but the man had been too full of himself to believe he would ever be caught. Pride went before a fall was not just a phrase to embroider on kitchen towels, Brent mused.

"Saunders wound up ruined, Jackson wound up free. Saunders's wife filed for divorce, took their little girl and disappeared to another state before the trial was even over." As he finished his narrative, he remembered the look in Saunders's eyes as he was being taken away. In that instant, Brent knew the man could have done this to him. An eye for an eye. His daughter for the one that Saunders had lost.

Except that Saunders was in prison.

Callie arrived at the same conclusion. "And since you were the presiding judge, he figured that you took away his life." She shook her head. "We need to find out just how long this guy's reach is."

She made a mental note to call Diaz with a series of questions for the prisoner just as they pulled up in front of Jackson's house.

It was more of a palace than a house, she thought, getting out. "Well, whatever went on at Saunders Computers certainly didn't hurt this guy."

"Until now," Brent commented grimly.

"Yeah."

They threaded their way past the hive of police personnel and investigators to the open entrance. Adams met them just as they crossed the threshold.

"Nice place," Callie commented.

"He had no one to share it with," Adams told her. "The man lived alone."

And now he didn't live at all, she thought. Aside from all the police activity, nothing appeared to be

out of place. The murderer hadn't been in here. Or
had seen no reason to touch anything.

His attention had been elsewhere, she concluded.

"Hence there was no one to report him missing,"
Brent was saying.

Adams nodded. From his expression, his annoyance at having the judge intrude on his territory had
dissipated. "No telling how long he would have lain
there if we hadn't found his car."

Callie shivered. Not sure of Jackson's complicity
in all this, she still pitied the man. To be so alone
that no one even noticed you were missing had to be
the worst of all possible scenarios.

"I don't even want to think about it." She looked
at Adams hopefully. "Did you find anything yet?"

He led the way into the study. There was a man
slumped forward at the desk, his head on the blotter.
From this distance, he appeared to be sleeping. Except that part of the top of his head was missing.
And a step closer brought the offensive smell of
death to them.

Walking into the room, Callie saw the pool of
blood beneath Jackson's head. "No signs of a struggle. No forced entry. Either this guy we're looking
for was very good—"

"Or Jackson knew his killer," Brent concluded.

"Or Jackson knew his killer," Adams agreed.
"Provided this is Jackson. Diaz has his DMV
photo."

"I know what he looks like," Brent volunteered,
moving forward.

"We can't move him until the CSI team finishes," Adams informed him.

Brent didn't hear as he squatted down beside the dead man. He didn't need to move him. He could tell by looking at the side of the murder victim's face. Jackson had a receding chin and a sandy-colored mustache meant to cover parts of a cleft lip that surgery hadn't been able to quite fix.

"It's Jackson."

Brent clenched his hands at his sides as he rose to his feet again. He looked at Callie. His inertia was threatening to drive him crazy. He couldn't keep following Callie around, seeing things secondhand. He needed to do something. "Look, can you get someone to drive me back to my house?"

Her hand on his arm, she moved him aside out of Adams's hearing range. "Sure. I understand." This was taking its toll on him emotionally. She shouldn't have brought him with her.

"No, I don't think you do. I'm going to go pay Saunders a visit," he told her. Somehow, some way, he felt that the man was at the bottom of all this. Brent needed to find out how.

"Diaz is already on his way," she reminded him. "We can go there once I'm finished here." She underscored the word *we*. There was no way she was going to let him go off on his own, not in his present emotional state.

Impatience threatened to do away with his better judgment and his control. "And just what is it that you're looking for here?"

She lifted one shoulder in response, not really aware of what she was seeking, only that she'd know when she saw it.

If she saw it.

"Something to talk to me."

Pulling on a pair of gloves, she moved about the study methodically, oblivious to the team already working there. They had their job; she had hers. She tried to imagine what had happened here a few days ago. There hadn't even been an attempt at pretending that this was a home invasion gone bad. Nothing had been taken.

Nothing appeared to be disturbed except for the man who had died in this room.

She shook her head, momentarily stumped. "This is like the rest of the house we just walked through. It looks like Ben Jackson was a very precise man who believed that everything had its place."

Feeling frustrated, Brent moved out of Callie's range and nearly backed up into the wastepaper basket. He saw it at the last moment and stopped himself. Looking down, he saw the broken frame inside the basket.

It looked as if it had been thrown there in anger. "Is this anything?"

The next moment, both Callie and Adams were behind him, looking down into the same wastepaper basket beside the dead man's desk. It was completely empty, except for the framed photograph and shattered glass.

"Maybe." At least, she hoped it was.

Taking the tangled frame and glass gingerly out of the basket, Callie carefully placed the contents of the basket on the coffee table. Behind her, the crime scene investigator had moved in to take another roll of photographs of the dead man.

The sound of the camera rhythmically clicking faded into the background as she looked at the photograph she had retrieved.

"Obviously happier times." The photograph was of Saunders and Jackson, both dressed in fishermen's garb. They were standing before a rustic-looking cabin. Saunders had his arm around a little girl.

She heard Brent's short intake of breath. He'd made the same mistake she had. At first glance the little girl looked almost identical to Rachel.

She turned toward Adams. "Have someone find out where this cabin is."

Adams took the photograph from her, the look in his eyes dubious. "Think that's important?"

"I don't know," she answered wearily. "But right now, until we know different, everything's important."

They went back to work, combing an almost spotless crime scene for clues.

He couldn't stay here.

Everywhere he turned, every place he looked, reminded him of Alice. He could almost hear her laughter echoing about the rooms.

The memory was too painful for him to handle.

He wanted to leave.

Needed to leave.

He and the little girl who was going to take Alice's place, to be his new Alice, needed to find a new place of their own.

That was why he couldn't sleep, couldn't think straight. Because of the memories that were here. Haunting him. He'd thought it would be all right here. That the memories would help him bridge what had been to what would be.

But they didn't. And he had to leave.

Except that he couldn't leave now. She was sick. He'd told her not to be, but she was anyway. He stood in the doorway of the bedroom, watching her sleep fitfully. She had a fever. Children couldn't control that kind of thing. They weren't responsible for things.

Not the way adults were.

Not the way Montgomery was.

But Montgomery had paid the ultimate price. And would continue paying it. All the days of his life. The son of a bitch would go on paying while he went on to enjoy what there was left of his own life. With his new Alice.

He knew they were looking for them. For her. But this time he'd be ready if they came. This time he wouldn't let them take him away from his little girl.

He'd kill both of them before that would happen.

Pacing, he looked at the clock as the minutes dragged along. It was hardly past five in the morning. He'd wanted to be on the road by now, but he couldn't. Not without risking Alice getting worse.

Maybe she'd be better by morning. Sure, why not? Kids got sick all the time, then bounced back before you knew it.

And then they could finally be on their way. Away from here. Away from everyone.

The thought pleased him, and he smiled to himself.

Hear that, Judge? We're going away from every-one. Away from you. You ruined my life. I'm just returning the favor.

Behind him he heard the little girl stirring. He hur-ried over to see if she'd finally woken up. The med-icine he'd given her had knocked her out for a long time.

Too long.

Chapter 14

"What the hell do you mean there's been a mistake?" Brent demanded, staring at Diaz. "How could this have happened?"

Their trip to Pelican State Prison, where Saunders had been sent, had been abruptly aborted before it began with Detective Diaz's unexpected return. On his way there, the detective had called ahead to the prison to arrange for the meeting when he'd been informed that he was too late.

Saunders was gone.

The moment he'd received the news, he'd made a U-turn and returned to Jackson's house. Now, caught in a circumstance beyond his control, Detective Ramon Diaz looked haplessly at the judge, then turned to Callie to run interference. None of this was his fault.

He recited what he'd been told. "According to the warden, this kind of garbage does happen. More often than anyone would like. There's a computer glitch, the wrong papers get processed and suddenly, the wrong man gets released."

Brent felt as if someone had just kicked him in the chest. It was surreal. Any minute now he was going to wake up, find out that this was a bad dream. All of it. Except for having been with Callie.

But he couldn't afford to focus on that now, even if it gave him the strength to see the rest of it through. He didn't have that luxury.

Because this wasn't a bad dream, it was real, it was happening. Somehow, through a whimsical act of fate, Saunders was free. Had been free for more than three weeks.

And there was no doubt in his mind that Saunders had his little girl.

Shifting restlessly, Brent scrubbed his hand over his face. "Saunders was a wizard when it came to computers, maybe he found a way to hack into the state prison system, get himself paroled."

Brent realized he was thinking out loud. And the how didn't matter. What mattered was that it was a reality. That Saunders was out there somewhere. With his little girl. There were too many fingers pointing in that direction for it to be merely a case of one coincidence on top of another.

Callie's brain was whizzing around with different theories. "Okay, let's go with this. Saunders sprang himself out of prison. He's ruined, penniless, his wife and daughter are gone." The coroner's team went past them with the body bag. She set her mouth grimly. "The only driving force in his life is revenge. Against the people who were instrumental in sending him away." She turned toward Adams. "Find out who the prosecuting attorney on the case was and send a couple of uniforms to his house to keep watch."

Brent shook his head. "Don't bother. Daryl Watson was the prosecutor. He died eighteen months ago of cancer."

Callie assimilated the information. "Robbing Saunders of the pleasure of doing away with him." She rerouted. "All right, Saunders gets out, finds a way to come up here and pay his old buddy Jackson a visit. Maybe Jackson is so stunned he lets him in, tries to make amends, whatever. Saunders kills him with his own gun." Adams had already told her the weapon was registered to Jackson. It just increased the irony. "He steals the Mercedes and comes to your neck of the woods," she looked at Brent, "to settle his last score."

"By kidnapping Rachel?" Why hadn't the man come after him? Why his daughter, Brent silently demanded. She was innocent. He was the one Saunders wanted.

"You said it yourself. His daughter looks just like Rachel in that photograph. In his mind, you caused him to lose his daughter. It's only fair that he take yours."

"Where? How? He abandoned the Mercedes," Brent reminded her.

"A man like Saunders always has a plan. He did that to throw us off. He knew we'd be looking for it. He probably had another car waiting in the vicinity. This was not haphazard, this was carefully thought out." She raised her eyes to Brent's. "Off the top of my head, my guess is that he'd be going someplace where he knew happier times."

He thought of the photograph in the wastepaper basket. "The cabin?"

"The cabin," she agreed. "Adams, how are we doing with finding out where this cabin is?"

Adams smiled. "I got one of our people to access county records. Jackson owns a cabin fifty miles north of here."

"Then that's where we'll go." There was some kind of an emotional connection to the cabin. Otherwise, there was no reason for the photograph to have been thrown away like that.

Adams hurried to keep pace with Callie and Brent as they headed back toward her car. "Here's the irony of it. The cabin used to belong to Saunders. Saunders had to sell it to pay his legal fees. Jackson scooped it up after Saunders was convicted."

Reaching her car, Callie shook her head. "Looks like Saunders wasn't the only heartless bastard in the lot."

Adrenaline was rushing through her veins, fueled by the coffee Diaz had mercifully shoved into her hand a second before she drove away from Jackson's house. Dawn had arrived sometime during their trip up here, gently stirring the rest of the world awake.

The cabin was only several yards ahead. There was a car parked to the side of the building. Someone was staying at the cabin. Saunders, she hoped.

Standing in the clearing with the woods on two sides and the lake as a backdrop, she saw all the elements of a peaceful, idyllic scene. The kind envisioned by vacationers desperate to get away from it all.

Except this one contained a kidnapper.

God willing, she added.

She and Brent had left her car with the other vehicles less than half a mile up the road. Backup was only a stone's throw away behind her, but she had decided that to rush the rustic building from all accessible sides could ultimately result in a tragedy. The cabin was exposed as would any group rushing it be. Seeing them coming for him, it would take Saunders less than a heartbeat to end the little girl's life.

In this case, Callie reasoned, less was more.

"Him?" Adams demanded, looking accusingly at the judge before shifting his attention back to Callie. It was obvious he had expected to be at her side. "Why are you taking him with you? You and super-judge expect to just walk right in there and if Saunders starts firing, the bullets will go flying off you?"

She knew that beneath the sarcastic tone, Adams was actually concerned about her safety. It wouldn't do to have his ex-partner killed right before his eyes without lifting a finger to prevent it.

They didn't have much time. She talked fast. "No. I'm hoping his desire for revenge keeps him from shooting at us until after he finishes gloating and rubbing the judge's face in it."

"And what's that supposed to do?" Adams growled, glaring at Diaz, who was fitting Brent with a bulletproof vest.

Callie finished strapping on her own vest, then slid her jacket over it. "Get us inside where hopefully we can keep Rachel from getting hurt." She looked at Brent. "That's going to be your job."

Adams was far from convinced. "So you expect to catch the bullets with your teeth?"

She patted his face, knowing that irritated him. She wanted him sharp, alert. And quick to act. "I expect to distract him so that he doesn't notice you making like the cavalry and coming in to the rescue." She began to go, then stopped and looked over her shoulder at Adams. "Just one thing."

"What?" he snapped.

"Don't make it the seventh cavalry."

His dark eyebrows drew together as he exchanged looks with Diaz, then glared back at Callie. "What's wrong with the seventh?"

"That was Custer's division," Brent put in. And they all knew what happened there, he thought.

That did it for Adams. He put his hand on Callie's shoulder to keep her from going. "Look, why don't I—"

She shrugged off his hand. Her tone was firm, although she was grateful for what he thought he was doing. Keeping her safe. It wasn't about her safety. It was about the safety of a little girl. "No, I'm primary."

But when she turned to go, she found Brent blocking her way.

He wanted to save his daughter. But he didn't want to risk the life of the woman he had come to care about a great deal. To him, it wasn't a trade-off. He wanted both.

"Callie, he's right."

Of all people, she hadn't expected him to turn on her. "I don't remember asking for an opinion poll." The moment was tense, tempers were on edge. She could feel hers flaring. They were wasting time here. "And you wouldn't be thinking that if I wasn't a woman."

The look in his eyes told her things he couldn't say out loud. Not here. Not yet.

Brent lowered his voice. "If you weren't a woman, I wouldn't have been thinking a lot of things."

She didn't have time for her mind to go there, to wonder what he was saying to her. To hope that it meant what she wanted it to. Right now she had a job to do, a child to rescue and a multiple killer to arrest. She was through debating. Squaring her shoulders, she moved forward. "Ready?"

He'd been ready from the first moment. "You don't have to ask."

Leaving the others behind, Callie and Brent kept to the cover of the brush as long as possible. But the last twenty feet was out in the open. There was a lake at the back of the cabin, the same lake that was in the photograph. She'd already sent two SWAT team members to make sure there wasn't a boat there, waiting to take Saunders and Rachel away.

She'd covered all the bases. Now it was time to run for home.

"What's the plan?" Crouching beside her, Brent looked out at the exposed terrain. "We just walk up to the front door and knock?"

Saunders could easily see them from any one of five windows facing front. Two on the first floor, three on the second.

"If he doesn't shoot one of us first, I jimmy it open." She spared him a glance. "It's all I got."

Brent nodded. The element of surprise was still on their side. Provided that Saunders didn't see them. "Let's go," Brent urged.

Hurrying the rest of the way in a zigzag pattern, in case Saunders wanted to take a shot at them from one of the windows, they miraculously made it to the front door without incident.

Miracle or not, Callie had an uneasy feeling as she worked to open the lock.

The lock gave. She took her service revolver out. "This is too easy," she whispered to Brent.

And it was. The moment the door opened, she saw that Saunders was standing there, a gun in his hand. He aimed it at her.

"Come on in," he taunted, waving them forward with his revolver. He took care to aim it at her again. "Think I didn't see you? I see everything." His eyes narrowed as he cocked his gun. "Drop your gun. Put it on the floor. Now," he ordered when she made no move to comply.

Callie had no choice. Never taking her eyes off him, she placed her weapon on the throw rug before Saunders. The man looked like hell, she thought. His eyes were bloodshot and his skin pallor was pasty. She was willing to bet he hadn't slept in a while. She'd seen an earlier photograph of Saunders in the judge's file. That man had looked dapper, smug. The man standing before her looked like his own grandfather.

"Give me the gun, Mr. Saunders," Callie coaxed softly. "Nobody else needs to get hurt."

Her words seemed to infuriate him. "You're wrong." For a second he shifted the gun to point at Brent. There was rage in his eyes. "He needs to be hurt. He needs to be hurt like he hurt me." His movements were jerky, spasmodic. Like a man tottering on the edge, about to fall. Or jump. "And he's going to be." Saunders's voice cracked. "I'm leaving here with Alice."

"Alice isn't here," Brent told him. Rage tinted Saunders's pasty complexion. He wanted to bait Saunders, to keep his attention focused on him, not Callie. There was no telling what the man was capable of in his present state of mind. "She left with her mother. But I know where she is. I can place a call and you can talk to her.''

For a moment Saunders's eyes brightened, but then, just as quickly, the light went out again.

''You're lying, you bastard. You don't know where she is. I tried to find her and I couldn't.'' All his computer expertise had failed him. Motioning them back, he stepped forward and picked up Callie's gun. ''Nobody knows where she is.'' He shoved Callie's gun into his belt. ''But that's all right, because I have a new Alice. I can start over again with her.'' The look on his face turned maniacal as he taunted Brent. ''Your little girl thinks I'm her new daddy, do you know that? I told her that you didn't want her anymore.''

Rachel knew better than that, Brent told himself. But she was only five. Had this monster brainwashed her? Made her believe that her father had abandoned her? Rage filled him.

''Where is she?'' he demanded.

Brent took a step toward the stairs. Nervous, shifting from foot to foot, Saunders pointed the gun he was holding at him.

''Get back, you bastard, she's mine now. There's nothing you can do about it.''

Callie felt her nerves fraying. How long did it take for Adams to make his way forward with the SWAT team? This maniac was liable to shoot Brent at any moment. She tried to divert his attention back to her.

Her voice was low, soft, kind. ''You're not well, Mr. Saunders. There are people who can help you.''

She took half a step forward, only to have him swing the barrel of his weapon on her.

The laugh was half-crazed and sent her flesh crawling. "Haven't you heard? God helps those who help themselves. And I'm helping myself."

The look in his eyes made Brent's blood run cold. He heard the weapon being cocked. It was aimed straight at Callie.

"Duck!" Brent cried.

Dropping down, Brent grabbed the edges of the throw rug and pulled it as hard as he could, yanking it out from beneath Saunders's feet.

Still clutching the gun, Saunders fell backward, just as Brent had calculated that he would. The shot went wild. Callie's gun fell from beneath his belt. Brent seized his one opportunity. He leaped on top of the man, struggling for possession of the weapon still in Saunders's hand.

Callie scrambled for her own weapon, which had flown halfway across the floor the moment Saunders had gone down. It was lodged under a seated coat-rack. Reaching beneath it as far as she could, her fingers came in contact with the muzzle. She felt as if her arm was coming out of its socket as she struggled for that extra inch that finally allowed her to secure the weapon.

With the gun in her hand, Callie was instantly on her feet. Spinning around, it took her a second to orient herself. Brent and Saunders were still tangled together.

Both hands on the weapon, she trained it on the kidnapper.

"Stop," she ordered. "Stop or I'll shoot."

The words were futile and she knew it before they were out of her mouth. Saunders, even in his present state of mind, must know that he had everything to lose if he surrendered. If he wanted to get revenge by kidnapping Rachel, and that was snatched away from him, then all he had left was killing the man who in his mind had caused his whole world to crumble for him.

Her heart was pounding as fear ate away at her. Any second now, the gun between the two men could discharge, killing Brent. They kept moving. Getting a clear shot at Saunders was next to impossible. But she had to get the man to stop before it was too late.

She did her best to try to aim the weapon at Saunders. "Surrender your weapon now, Saunders. I don't want to shoot you, but I will."

The next movement took her by complete surprise. As if the sound of her voice had suddenly set him off, Saunders twisted around, let loose with a wild, guttural scream that sounded as if it was half animal, half human and lunged for her.

Callie hit the back of her head on the floor as she went down.

Everything went spinning and she struggled for consciousness. Her gun was crushed between them, her hand bent backward at an excruciating angle. Pain shot through her arm.

And then Saunders's hands were wrapped around

her throat. Screaming obscenities at her, he tightened his grasp, squeezing, cutting off her air. There was a wild throbbing in her brain as she tried to claw his fingers away.

She was getting light-headed. Somewhere far away, there was a strange popping noise and then a huge weight fell on top of her, crushing her. The next moment the weight was being dragged off her, and then she felt herself being lifted.

Desperate for air, Callie gulped it in, filling her lungs, trying to focus.

With effort, she could make out Brent's face. He was holding her against him. His eyes looked worried. "Are you all right?"

The room came back into focus. Saunders lay in a heap on the floor, with blood everywhere. On the floor, on her. On Brent because he'd held her to him.

Her heart racing, Callie managed to nod. It took her a second before she could talk. "You?"

Relief filled him as he brushed the hair away from her face. She looked shaken, but otherwise unharmed. "I'm all right."

Just then the door behind them flew open, and the room was filled with helmeted policeman. Adams and Diaz were at the head of the group.

"That would be the cavalry," she breathed. Still holding on to Brent's hand, she pressed her free hand to her forehead, trying to pull herself together. That had been close, very close.

She looked at the SWAT team and quipped, "I'm afraid you're all dressed up with nowhere to go."

She nodded toward the prone body. "He won't be giving you any trouble."

The other detective immediately crossed to the man on the floor to examine him for any signs of life. Callie heard questions coming at her from all directions, melding together and swallowed up by more noise. She held her hand up. "Hold it, let me get my bearings here."

Brent looked at her. There was a gash on her forehead. "I'm calling for the paramedics."

"They don't do bearings," she murmured. And then she stopped.

Brent searched her face. "What's the matter?"

Callie said nothing. She pointed behind him. To the top of the stairs. Where a small, frightened figure was staring down at the activity below, clutching at the banister with both hands.

"Daddy?"

Brent's heart leaped up into his throat, as Rachel looked down at him. Her expression was timid, as if she was afraid that this was just another dream. That she'd wake up and find that she was still not home.

"Daddy?" she cried again, louder this time.

He took the stairs two at a time, reaching his daughter in less time than it took her to repeat his name. Scooping her up into his arms, he held her close, a sob threatening to tear loose from his throat.

"It's me, baby, it's me. It's Daddy," he assured her. He never wanted to let her go again.

Rachel was crying, holding on to him for dear life as he came back down the stairs with her. "The man said you didn't want me anymore. That you weren't my daddy anymore.''

Coming to the landing, Brent kissed his daughter's hair, her cheeks, her forehead. Tears threatened to undo him. Somehow he managed to hold them back, but they shimmered in his eyes as he looked at Callie, unable to speak the gratitude that vibrated in his heart.

"I will always want you, Rachel. And I will always, always be your daddy.''

Callie stepped back, wiping away tears with the back of her hand. Giving Brent a moment alone with his daughter.

"You okay, Callie?'' Adams asked.

She rubbed her throat. It was going to be raw for a few days, she suspected. And the gash on her forehead was going to need attention. But all things considered, she was wonderful.

"Better than okay,'' she told him. "This one has a happy ending.'' She looked over toward the man who'd inexplicably turned the sum of his wrath on her. Maybe in some way she reminded him of his wife, she thought. It didn't matter now. "Is he—''

Adams nodded. "He won't be kidnapping any more little girls. Saunders is dead.''

She nodded, numb and relieved at the same time. "Like I said, a happy ending.''

"What happened?''

"He lunged at me. Tried to choke me.''

Adams looked at her, puzzled. "Then how did you—''

''Shoot him?'' she guessed at his question. ''I didn't. The judge did.''

''You're kidding.''

''Nope.'' She looked back at Brent cradling his daughter. ''I guess you never know what you have inside you until your back's against the wall.''

''Amen to that,'' Adams agreed.

Chapter 15

"But I don't want to go to the hospital," Rachel cried. Her eyes were wide as she pulled on her father's hand, trying to get him to come away. They were outside the cabin. Behind them, the rear doors of the ambulance were opened and the paramedics stood waiting to take her to the nearest hospital. There was real terror in Rachel's eyes as she looked up at him, pleading, "I want to go home."

Brent looked torn between doing what he knew was necessary and not wanting to cause his little girl any more anxiety. Callie could see that he was about to give in to the child, at least for the time being. She glanced at the paramedics before she crouched down to the little girl's level.

"I don't like hospitals, either," she confided to Rachel, her voice low. She indicated the gash over her left eye. "But they tell me I have to have this cut taken care of."

She smiled encouragingly, slowly taking hold of Rachel's free hand. For a moment they seemed to form a unit, she and Brent and his daughter. But she couldn't allow her thoughts to go there. Especially not now. Not when they were wrapping everything up.

"Tell you what," Callie continued, her voice guileless, "if you hold my hand while the doctor takes care of me, I'll hold yours while he takes care of you. Do we have a deal?"

Rachel pressed her lips together, considering. She glanced at her father then back at Callie.

"Please?" Callie coaxed hopefully. "It'll be a big favor to me."

A shy smile curved her mouth. The small head bobbed up and down. "Okay. I'll hold your hand."

"Great, I feel better already."

Very slowly she drew Rachel over to the ambulance. Then, holding her by the waist, she placed the little girl inside before getting in herself. Only then did she allow herself to look at Brent. There was an expression on his face she couldn't read. She tried to keep her voice cheery.

"C'mon, 'Dad,'" she urged. "You get to ride back here, too."

"As if you could stop me," Brent commented, getting in.

As one of the paramedics shut the double doors

on them, Callie looked at Rachel. She wanted to keep the girl distracted until they reached the hospital.

"You know, I bet if you ask the driver nicely, he might let you press the siren as we go." Turning, she looked at the paramedic. "What do you say, driver? Can she press the siren?"

The burly man grinned at Brent's daughter. "Sure, come on up here."

Rachel scrambled up to the front seat and was safely strapped in before the driver started up the ambulance. The other paramedic rode in the back with them. He eyed Callie's wound like a chef waiting for a pot to rebel and boil over.

Brent tried to relax and found that it was next to impossible. He'd packed in twenty years' worth of living in the last few days and it had definitely taken a toll on him. There was just so long a man could live on a constant surge of adrenaline. He struggled for equilibrium, telling himself that from now on, things were going to be settling down.

Better than that, they were going to be good.

He looked at Callie. "You didn't tell me you were good with kids."

Now that it was over, she could feel the numbness leaving her body. It was starting to ache. All over. She'd taken one hell of a spill when Saunders had lunged at her.

Leaning against the side wall, she slanted a glance in Brent's direction. "As I recall, the subject never came up. I love kids, why?"

It was an area he felt compelled to proceed

through slowly, as if in a minefield. But it was a minefield he was determined to cross.

"I didn't think kids went with your line of work."

Callie laughed softly. It hurt her ribs. "Wrong. Kids most definitely go with my line of work. Kids are what my work is all about. Keeping the world safe so that they can grow up unafraid and happy." They heard Rachel laugh gleefully as the siren went off. "She's a wonderful little girl."

Pure pleasure shone in his eyes as he looked toward the front. "I always thought so."

"Would you have more?" The question had just popped up on her lips and she knew she shouldn't ask. It might give him the idea that she was fishing for something. Nothing could be further from the truth. She knew when to put away her equipment and withdraw.

"In a heartbeat—" He looked at her, remembering what he had felt when she'd taken Rachel's hand. There was no doubt in his mind that Callie would make a wonderful mother. "If the opportunity arose."

Was he putting her on notice? Or warning her that she wasn't the opportunity? Her head began to ache, joining the symphony of pain playing over the rest of her body.

Don't go there, she upbraided herself. They'd saved Rachel and that was more than enough for one day.

"Oh," was all she ventured. With a satisfied smile, Callie leaned further back in her chair, counting the minutes until they reached the hospital. Her temple stung and she had one killer of a headache.

The warmth she was feeling at a job well done more than helped balance it out.

The emergency room physician signed off on her, but only when she promised to go straight home. The alternative was to remain in the hospital overnight for observation, something she wasn't about to do. Callie said the words with her fingers mentally crossed. She stayed in the hospital only long enough to keep her promise to Rachel and hold her hand during the little girl's own examination.

The pediatrician who was called down to attend to her pronounced Rachel to be remarkably well, considering the ordeal she'd gone through. He said something about the resilience of children as he made notes on the chart, discharging her into her father's care.

By that time Rachel was dancing from foot to foot, a pony anxiously waiting for the starting gate to be opened. "Now we can go home?" she asked hopefully, turning her small, shining face up to her father.

"Now we can go home," he echoed. Unable to resist indulging himself, Brent picked his daughter up and carried her down the hall.

Rachel wiggled a little. "I can walk, Daddy." But her protest didn't carry a whole lot of conviction with it. She was happy to be back in her father's arms.

"Humor me," he told her.

Puzzled, she looked at Callie, who was walking beside her father, for an explanation.

Callie laughed. The little girl was a sponge. Very much the way her own father had claimed she was at that age. "That means make him happy and let him do this."

"Oh. Okay," Rachel said brightly. She threaded her fingers through each other around her father's neck. She looked into his face, her voice small. "I missed you, Daddy."

Emotion welled up in his throat, choking him. "And I missed you."

Her voice grew smaller as she confided to him, "I knew you'd come for me. He said you wouldn't, but I knew you would."

Her faith in him overwhelmed Brent. He was so relieved that he hadn't failed his daughter. And it was all because of Callie.

"And I always will," he promised.

Time to go, Callie thought as she followed Brent and his daughter through the electronic doors. Activity hummed all around them. She saw only Brent.

Gently she laid her hand on his shoulder, drawing his attention. "Detective Diaz will get you home."

The cold air stung his face as he turned to look at Callie. "What about you?"

She couldn't resist moving Rachel's long hair over her shoulder. The kid was going to be fine.

You did a good job, Cavanaugh, she congratulated herself.

If something was stirring within her chest, feeling

strange, feeling sad, she wasn't going to pay attention to it. "What about me?"

"Aren't you coming?"

"The case is over, Judge." She lightly rubbed her hand against Rachel's cheek. "And I've got a mountain of paperwork to file."

"Can't it wait?"

She shook her head. *Don't make this any harder than it is, Brent.*

"Afraid not. If I leave it, it'll only find a way to multiply." She smiled at the little girl. "It was wonderful to finally meet you in person, Rachel. Take good care of your daddy." She had no idea why her heart ached as she added, "He loves you very, very much."

"I know," Rachel responded brightly, tightening her arms around his neck.

Go, go! she urged herself. Callie turned on her heel and began to walk away.

"The E.R. doctor said to go home," Brent called after her.

Callie glanced over her shoulder. "The E.R. doctor doesn't have my captain breathing down his neck."

She didn't trust herself to say anything else, or to linger even for one more moment like an unwanted guest after the party was over. Her business with Brent was concluded. Without the need to be together, she would only remind him of the terror he'd lived through, waiting to find out if his daughter was alive or dead.

It was best for both of them if she made this clean break for them. She hurried over to Adams, who was waiting by his vehicle. If he was surprised to see her coming his way, he didn't let on.

"Get me back to the office."

"You sure?"

She kept her face forward, not wanting to risk looking back. "I'm sure."

A clean break might be better, Callie thought hours later, after the day had long since dragged itself to an end and she was dragging herself up the walk to her apartment, but it certainly didn't feel better. What it felt like was hell.

So did coming home to her small apartment. She flipped on the light switch next to the front door. The ensuing illumination did nothing to dispel the mood that was hanging over her.

The apartment felt lonelier tonight. As lonely as it had when she'd walked into it that first night she realized Kyle would no longer be part of her life.

Callie stripped off her jacket, then her service revolver with its holster. Her body ached. She tried to concentrate on the pain there and not the darkness surrounding her heart.

It didn't help.

She'd done it again. She'd gone and left her defenses down, allowed her feelings to get loose. Allowed herself to fall for someone.

How hard could you fall in just a few days, she

tried to argue, clinging to rationality. But she knew the answer to that. Hard. Very hard.

The time line didn't matter, and if it did, legally it had started years ago. On a dance floor for a fund-raiser. She sighed as she plopped down on her sofa. It sighed along with her.

The blinking light on her answering machine caught her eye. She decided to ignore it. She didn't feel like talking to anyone tonight.

Needing noise, she reached for the remote control and turned on the television set, not bothering to see what station it was on. The low drone of voices was all she required. It didn't even matter if the program was in English or not, as long as there was no silence to bounce her thoughts around in.

The phone rang. Murmuring an oath under her breath, wishing everyone would leave her alone for a little while, she let her machine pick it up.

"Callie, if you don't answer me, I'm coming over."

He would, too, she thought. With a sigh she reached for the cordless receiver.

"Hi, Dad, here I am, answering. No need for you to come over."

"You weren't here for breakfast this morning." Andrew Cavanaugh's voice wasn't judgmental. It sounded as if he was merely stating a fact the way he might have once read from his notepad. He liked having his brood around.

Weary, Callie dragged her hand through her hair. Maybe she was being needlessly stubborn. Maybe she should take one of those painkillers the E.R. doctor had given her and just let oblivion claim her.

But she knew that it wouldn't do a damn thing for the real pain she was feeling. When she woke up, it would still be there.

"I've missed mornings before, Dad," she reminded him.

"Yes, you have." His voice was patient. "But you usually called during the day to say why."

There were times when having a big family felt confining. The second the thought was formed, she felt guilty. Droves of people would kill to have what she had and she knew it. "The case heated up."

"And?"

She smiled to herself. You could take the badge away from the policeman, but you couldn't take the policeman away from the badge. "And we found her."

"Alive?"

She was so involved in the case, she'd forgotten that everyone else didn't know the details of the outcome. "Yes, thank God. Rachel's home now with her father. And mother," Callie added after a beat.

Her father was silent for a moment. She knew he was doing the father thing. Reading into her words. Reading her mind. "Is everything okay, Callie?"

"Sure," she said a little too quickly, even for her own ear.

"You wouldn't be lying to your old dad now, would you?"

She picked up on the words she wanted and ran

with them. "I don't have an old dad. My dad's young and virile and a pain in the butt sometimes."

Andrew laughed heartily. She hadn't answered his question, but he knew to leave it alone. Privacy was something they all respected. Up to a point. "I just worry about my kids. No law against that. See you tomorrow?"

She feigned surprise at the question. "What, miss two days in a row and risk being drawn and quartered?" And then her voice softened. "I'll be there, Dad."

She hung up and stared at the phone. It was the first time she'd lied to her father since her teens. Everything wasn't all right. But it would be. By and by.

The phone rang again.

The man just didn't give up, did he? she thought with a sigh. Jerking the receiver back up, she said shortly, "I said I'd be there, so I'll be there. Do you want it confirmed in blood?"

There was a pause on the other end. "No. But how did you know I was going to invite you over? You didn't tell me you were clairvoyant."

Brent.

She could feel her heart leaping up, then thundering against her bruised ribs.

"Oh. Brent." For a second she was completely flustered. Her mind went blank. And then she pulled herself together, doing her best not to sound like the idiot she felt. "I'm not. That is, I thought you were my father calling again." Her tongue was tangling, tripping her up. She tried again. "He wanted to know if I was planning on coming to breakfast tomorrow."

"That's right, you missed going there this morning."

For the very best of reasons, she thought. She blew out a breath, feeling a little more in control. "How's Rachel?"

"Great. Asleep." She wasn't the only one fumbling, she thought. A smile spread across her lips as she listened. "I don't know if I ever said thank you."

She pulled the morning's events back into focus before answering. "No, not in so many words, but you didn't have to. Seeing you and Rachel reunited again said it all."

"Still, thank you. From the bottom of my heart. I'll never be able to begin to repay you." His voice was warm against her ear. "Look, I'm having a little party tomorrow to celebrate Rachel's homecoming. We'd like you to be there."

We.

He was talking about Jennifer and him, she realized. Had this whole terrible incident brought his ex-wife and Brent together?

Damn it, it's none of your business, Cavanaugh. And this is better for Rachel, she argued silently. Children needed parents. One of each. In one house.

Still, she didn't have to be there to see this particular pair of parents. She knew she wasn't up to it. "I'm afraid I'll have to pass, Your Honor. I've still got a lot of work to catch up on and—"

He didn't let her finish. "Rachel's going to be very disappointed."

Callie laughed shortly. She needed to cut her losses and pull back now, even though it was already too late. "She has you and her mother. I don't think she'll really miss me."

"Well, she has me." Brent sounded just the slightest bit puzzled. "But Jennifer's already caught a plane for home. She left early this afternoon."

"She caught—" Stunned, Callie tried to make sense out of what she was hearing. "But you said 'we.'"

"Yes, we. Rachel and I." His laugh was low, curling its way into her stomach. Just where she didn't need it to be. "What did you think I meant?"

"You and Jennifer. I thought the two of you got back together again."

"What gave you that idea?" Was it her imagination, or did he sound a little annoyed by her assumption? "Is that why you said no?"

"No, I really do have paperwork, I, um—" She was running out of steam. And out of the desire to keep pushing him away.

"I wish I was there right now," he said.

I do, too, but probably for a whole different reason than you. Callie kept her voice mild as she asked, "Why?"

"So I could see your nose growing. You're lying, Detective Cavanaugh. And really doing a very poor job of it."

She couldn't suppress the grin, but since she was alone, she figured there was no harm in it. "I'll work on it."

"Work on it when you come over tomorrow," he told her. His voice left no room for argument this time. "Six o'clock. Sharp."

Maybe it was her imagination, but the apartment looked just a touch brighter to her. Maybe there'd been a surge in the electricity she hadn't noticed. "Is there a penalty for being late?"

Brent laughed again. "I'll let you know when you get here."

"All right, you're on." Hanging up, Callie found she couldn't stop smiling.

By the time she drove up to Brent's house, she'd had close to twenty-four hours to talk herself out of smiling. She was just the detective on record who had helped solve the case, nothing more. There was no reason to think that anything had changed from yesterday.

It hadn't. The case was closed. And they both had lives to get on with. Apart.

There were a great many cars parked along the circular driveway as she approached. Too many.

Her car's engine still running, Callie debated turning the vehicle around and going home. He'd never miss her amid all these people. And she had already said her goodbyes. Why prolong the inevitable?

Making up her mind, she circled the driveway and began to pull out again.

"You can't leave until after you've arrived."

Startled, she looked out the passenger side. The window was down partially. Just enough so that she could hear Brent. He was walking quickly beside the car, matching its pace.

Where had he come from?

She ignored her scrambling pulse. "Why aren't you inside with your guests?"

"Because I've been standing out here on the front lawn, waiting for the only guest who counts to arrive."

She had the car down to barely a crawl, but it was still moving. The opportunity for flight comforted her. "Me?"

"You." He pointed to the left. "Pull your car over there, Detective, I need to talk to you."

She didn't know how to read that. He sounded almost stern. "Officially?"

He shrugged. "Officially, unofficially, any way you want to call it."

She did as she was told, leaving the car parked in the center of the circular driveway. By her count, she was blocking at least four other cars. Brent didn't seem to notice, or if he did, he didn't seem to care.

As she got out of the car, he took her hands in his. She was surprised to feel how cold they were.

"You should get inside," she told him, nodding toward the house behind him. It was lit up like a Christmas tree, and even with the windows closed, she could hear the sound of laughter. "Your hands are freezing."

His eyes washed over her, making her warm, before he answered. "They always get that way when I'm faced with something that scares the hell out of me."

She hadn't a clue what he was talking about. "And that is?"

"Hearing the word no."

It still made no sense. Callie cocked her head, curious. Unable to fathom anything that would frighten the judge now that his daughter was alive and safe. "In response to?"

"My question."

It was like pulling teeth. "Which is?"

He searched her face first, looking for a sign that he wasn't about to make a colossal fool of himself. That she did feel the way he'd told himself she felt. The way he felt. And that her reticence to be here was due to cold feet and not something else.

"Damn it, Judge, you've got to say it first. I don't want to be out of order." And what she really didn't want was to jump to conclusions. Because they certainly were jumping at her.

"Callie Cavanaugh, would I be completely out of line if I asked you to marry me?"

Callie's mouth dropped open. She'd thought he was going to ask her for a date, not for her hand and the rest of her in marriage.

For a moment, she could only stare at him. And then, finally, she found her tongue. "That depends."

Brent braced himself. He'd gone too far to back down. Not that he wanted to. "On what?"

This had come out of nowhere. The way he'd
made love to her had all the tenderness she could
have ever wished for, but she wasn't all that expe-
rienced when it came to men. She was afraid she was
reading things into it she'd wanted to be there.

And God forbid he was laboring under some kind
of emotional overload. "On whether you're asking
me out of some misguided sense of gratitude, or—"

"Or—" he coaxed, still holding her hands.

Taking a deep breath, she took the plunge. "Or
because you love me."

His eyes smiled into hers. Stirring her soul. "B.
Definitely B."

He loved her? He *loved* her? It didn't seem possible. She knew she wasn't going to believe it until
she heard it. Maybe not even then. "Oh, no, you
can't just spout a letter at me. You have to say it."

"Because I love you," he told her softly. "Because I've been in love with you for a very long time.
Because coming home and knowing you weren't going to be part of my life anymore was too painful a
thing for me to contemplate. You gave me back my
daughter and I will always be grateful, but that's not
a reason to want to marry someone, Callie. I want to
marry you because you're you. You're good with
Rachel, you're good with me." And then he grinned.
"And on top of all that, you've got killer legs."

She felt herself beaming, inside and out. "I'd say
that was good enough."

Oh, no, she didn't get off that easy. He needed to

hear the same words she did, he thought. "What else do you say?"

"Yes."

He waited. "And?" he prodded.

Could a person feel this wonderful and still live? "Double yes?"

"Callie."

She laughed, then withdrawing her hands, she threaded them around his neck. The wind had picked up, but she didn't care. She was warm all over. "Your Honor, if you don't know by now that I'm in love with you, then you're not nearly as shrewd as rumor says you are."

"Sometimes," he acknowledged, his voice brimming with the love he felt for her, "rumors are true."

"Amen to that," she murmured just before he kissed her.

* * * * *

*Don't miss the exciting continuation of
Marie Ferrarella's miniseries in
Intimate Moments, CAVANAUGH JUSTICE:
CRIME AND PASSION (IM1256)
Available November 2003*

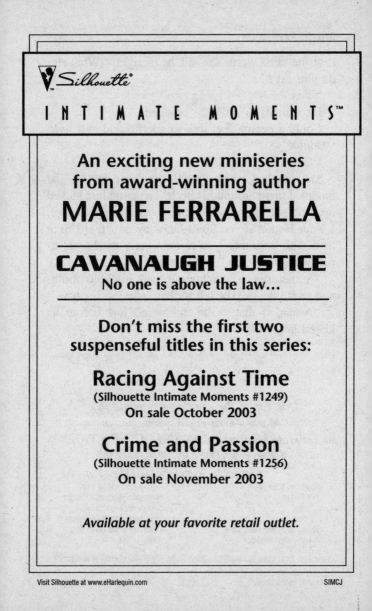

Your opinion is important to us! Please take a few moments to share your thoughts with us about your experiences with Harlequin and Silhouette books. Your comments will be very useful in ensuring that we deliver books you love to read.
Please take a few minutes to complete the questionnaire, then send it to us at the address below.

Send your completed questionnaires to:
Harlequin/Silhouette Reader Survey, P.O. Box 9046, Buffalo, NY 14269-9046

1. As you may know, there are many different lines under the Harlequin and Silhouette brands. Each of the lines is listed below. Please check the box that most represents your reading habit for each line.

Line	Currently read this line	Do not read this line	Not sure if I read this line
Harlequin American Romance	❑	❑	❑
Harlequin Duets	❑	❑	❑
Harlequin Romance	❑	❑	❑
Harlequin Historicals	❑	❑	❑
Harlequin Superromance	❑	❑	❑
Harlequin Intrigue	❑	❑	❑
Harlequin Presents	❑	❑	❑
Harlequin Temptation	❑	❑	❑
Harlequin Blaze	❑	❑	❑
Silhouette Special Edition	❑	❑	❑
Silhouette Romance	❑	❑	❑
Silhouette Intimate Moments	❑	❑	❑
Silhouette Desire	❑	❑	❑

2. Which of the following best describes why you bought *this book?* One answer only, please.

the picture on the cover	❑	the title	❑
the author	❑	the line is one I read often	❑
part of a miniseries	❑	saw an ad in another book	❑
saw an ad in a magazine/newsletter	❑	a friend told me about it	❑
I borrowed/was given this book	❑	other: _____	❑

3. Where did you buy *this book?* One answer only, please.

at Barnes & Noble	❑	at a grocery store	❑
at Waldenbooks	❑	at a drugstore	❑
at Borders	❑	on eHarlequin.com Web site	❑
at another bookstore	❑	from another Web site	❑
at Wal-Mart	❑	Harlequin/Silhouette Reader Service/through the mail	❑
at Target	❑		
at Kmart	❑	used books from anywhere	❑
at another department store or mass merchandiser	❑	I borrowed/was given this book	❑

4. On average, how many Harlequin and Silhouette books do you buy at one time?

I buy _____ books at one time ❑
I rarely buy a book ❑   MRQ403SIM-1A

5. How many times per month do you shop for any *Harlequin and/or Silhouette* books?
One answer only, please.

1 or more times a week	❑	a few times per year	❑
1 to 3 times per month	❑	less often than once a year	❑
1 to 2 times every 3 months	❑	never	❑

6. When you think of your ideal heroine, which *one* statement describes her the best?
One answer only, please.

She's a woman who is strong-willed	❑	She's a desirable woman	❑
She's a woman who is needed by others	❑	She's a powerful woman	❑
She's a woman who is taken care of	❑	She's a passionate woman	❑
She's an adventurous woman	❑	She's a sensitive woman	❑

7. The following statements describe types or genres of books that you may be
interested in reading. Pick *up to 2 types* of books that you are most interested in.

I like to read about truly romantic relationships	❑
I like to read stories that are sexy romances	❑
I like to read romantic comedies	❑
I like to read a romantic mystery/suspense	❑
I like to read about romantic adventures	❑
I like to read romance stories that involve family	❑
I like to read about a romance in times or places that I have never seen	❑
Other: _____	❑

*The following questions help us to group your answers with those readers who are
similar to you. Your answers will remain confidential.*

8. Please record your year of birth below.
19 ____

9. What is your marital status?

single ❑   married ❑   common-law ❑   widowed ❑
divorced/separated* ❑

10. Do you have children 18 years of age or younger currently living at home?
yes ❑   no ❑

11. Which of the following best describes your employment status?
employed full-time or part-time ❑   homemaker ❑   student ❑
retired ❑   unemployed ❑

12. Do you have access to the Internet from either home or work?
yes ❑   no ❑

13. Have you ever visited eHarlequin.com?
yes ❑   no ❑

14. What state do you live in?
_____

15. Are you a member of Harlequin/Silhouette Reader Service?
yes ❑   Account # _____   no ❑   MRQ403SIM-1B

If you enjoyed what you just read,
then we've got an offer you can't resist!

Take 2 bestselling love stories FREE!
Plus get a FREE surprise gift!

Silhouette®

COMING NEXT MONTH